COME WINTER

COME WINTER

****

EVAN HUNTER

Doubleday & Company, Inc., Garden City, New York

All of the characters in this book are fictitious, and
any resemblance to actual persons, living or dead
is purely coincidental.

This is for Mary Vann

ONE

FODERMAN

Sandy was in the lead.

She skied around each bend in the trail like a lunatic, long blond hair flying out behind her, dark-blue shiny parka reflecting sun and sky, jeans wet with snow—"Yaaaaaaaaaaaah!" she yelled, and went flashing around another curve and out of sight. David, immediately behind her, made the same tight turn and disappeared behind the same clump of snow-laden pines. Some ten yards above them, I was suddenly alone on the steep trail, the mountain empty and still, not a whisper of wind, not a branch crackling, the only sound the chatter of my skis and the reverberating boom of stark-naked terror.

Don't let anyone tell you fear doesn't have a noise all its own, and a smell of dust besides. I once mentioned that to my friendly neighborhood shrink, Dr. Krakauer, and he said, "Ahh, yes, Peter? Und vhy precisely does it zmell of dust, eggs-actly?" It smelled of dust right that minute, dust that rose suffocatingly in my throat. Peter, I told myself, you are going to take a flying leap over one of these moguls and break your neck. (Ahh, yes, Peter? Und vot eggs-actly are moguls? Moguls are closely spaced, hard-packed mounds of snow,

Dr. Krakauer.) Or else I was going to miss the turn Sandy and David had just negotiated with Grace and Style (those well-known vaudeville performers) and end up in the hospital with multiple fractures of the skull. God, I was scared.

The turn was coming up too fast, preceded by a pair of immense moguls that stoutly defended a ribbon of trail as narrow as the Khyber Pass. I chose the mogul on the left, dipped, swung up over it with my heart in the hood of my parka, yanked myself around it like a rank beginner, almost crossed the tips of my skis, almost flew headlong through them to fulfill the prophecy of busted cerebellum, managed to right myself, and came around the corner with arms flailing, poles thrashing, boots apart, knees shaking—and there ahead, not ten feet from where I clattered awkwardly into view, David and Sandy stood serenely by the side of the trail, watching. Breathlessly, barely in control, I skidded to a snow-spraying stop that almost knocked over both of them, not to mention myself.

"What kept you, Peter?" Sandy said, dead-panned.

"Thought you'd never get here," David said.

"Very funny," I said. "What's the name of this trail? Death's Row?"

"Suicide Gulch," Sandy said.

"Hangman's Noose," David said.

"Ready to go?" Sandy said.

"Just *hold* it a second!" I said, and both jackasses burst into hysterical laughter. I merely ignored them. I checked my bindings, adjusted my hood, blew my nose, fussed with my zippers and fidgeted with my gloves until I figured they were all laughed out. Then, with deliberate calm and considerable courage, I dug in both poles, pushed off, and headed straight down the fall line like Jean Claude Killy on a Sunday outing.

Behind me, I heard Sandy give a small yelp and take off in pursuit.

I skied beautifully, I must admit it.

It was one of those incredibly clear bright days, the sky impeccably blue and flawless, the trail fast, winding between tall shady stands of pine and spruce. Confident now, determined to race Sandy's tail off even if it meant soaring like an eagle over moguls, blazing fresh trails through the woods, or booming the mountain nonstop, I experienced that sometime sense (but oh so rare!) of oneness with the terrain, snow and body acting and reacting subtly and surely, southern sun on my face, the wind of my own speed, hushed whisper of skis, twisting and bending and gliding like a ballet dancer on a frozen cloud.

There was a solitary skier on the trail ahead of me, a dumpy little man in a long black parka, black woolen hat with a little orange pompom. I skied around him effortlessly, passing him on the left, giving him wide berth, and then studied the terrain ahead and saw a flat stretch of wide-open, almost level ground glowing in sunlight, the snow glittering with miniscule pink and blue and yellow crystals. I carved a wide turn, came to a stop, and then turned to look up the mountain, striking the same nonchalant pose Sandy and David had earlier affected. Above me, the skier in black was having a little difficulty, picking his way cautiously and gingerly down the trail, flanked on either side by giant trees in painful silhouette against the sky.

A saffron banner suddenly streaked into view at the crest of the slope. Head bent, blond hair flying, hips and knees and poles working, Sandy darted and danced down the difficult trail, David close behind her, while below the skier in black mustered his courage and pushed himself over the top of a mogul and started a descent in something closely resembling a beginner's snowplow. Sandy's speed was dazzling. She used the fall line like a thread pulled tight between her body and the bottom of the mountain, spotting the skier in black a scant second after she came over the top of the mogul he had just navigated. He must have seen her in the same instant. Both swerved, Sandy to the left, the other skier to the right, toward the woods. Standing below, witnessing all of it, I simply could not believe what happened next.

Instead of stopping (he was surely moving slow enough to stop), instead of *trying* to stop, even *sitting* to stop, the skier in black continued impossibly and inexorably toward the woods. The effect from below was nearly comical. Here was this dumpy little man moving in slow motion toward the looming trees, but in such a deliberate way that it seemed he was hoping to find a warming hut in there, and maybe a nice cup of hot chocolate besides. David, speeding past, turned his head for a quick look at this athletic phenomenon, just as the little man with the orange pompom on his hat skied slowly, steadfastly, and directly into the forest, crashing obliviously through hanging branches in a shower of falling snow, disappearing entirely from sight.

Sandy pulled to a stop beside me.

"Guy up there just skied into the woods," I said.

"Yeah?" she said, and looked up the slope.

David, grinning, coming down toward us, yelled, "Hey, did you see *that?*"

"I missed it," Sandy said.

"Guy skied right into the woods there," David said.

"Maybe he *prefers* skiing in the woods," Sandy said, and shrugged.

"We'd better get the Ski Patrol," I said.

"Yeah," David said.

"Last one to the bottom sucks," Sandy said.

It was later that we discovered the skier's name was Emmanuel Schwartz, and that he had broken his leg in three places when he went off the trail into the deep snow.

I had never heard of Semanee Peak until Sandy's call at the beginning of December. When the phone rang, I was drinking a beer with an egg in it, my favorite antidote for the thrice-weekly, fifty-minute hours I spent with the inquisitive Dr. Krakauer, a man eager to discover the cause of my now-famous recurring nightmare. My usual pattern was to come back to the apartment after my 4:10 sessions (Tuesdays, Wednesdays, Fridays), kick off my loafers, crack open an egg, drop it into a cold glass of Heineken's truth serum (which I'd learned to drink on Greensward, lo, those many summers past), toast the mad physician's determination, and then swallow the egg whole, pretending it was his left eyeball, and washing it down with beer. I would then collapse on my own friendlier couch before tackling my schoolwork. School was N.Y.U. My apartment was on Lex and Twenty-third. Dr. Crackers had his office on Ninety-sixth and Madison. So much for geography.

Old Sandy was calling from Bennington, and telling me in a rush that she had heard of a great place in the heart of America's vast snow country, and wouldn't it be great if the three of us could go out there skiing for the holidays. I told her immediately that I didn't particularly care for the new voice she was cultivating, a phony breathless murmur, far inferior to her natural voice, which itself was deep and resonant, but which modulated sometimes into a high, exuberant girlish squeal that reminded me of those days five years ago, when we had tried to train a gull (and succeeded) and sworn loyalty to each other, and spent together the best summer of our lives. But Sandy at twenty was determined to develop a more sophisticated image, I suppose, even if it

meant lowering her voice to a barely audible whisper and
sounding somewhat like a boozy whore in a Third Avenue
bar. As far as I was concerned, she was quite sophisticated
enough, as slender and leggy as she'd been at fifteen, with narrow hips and tiny breasts that were perfect for today's breezy
bra-less look, long pale-blond hair framing a face that had
lengthened somewhat in maturity, vivid blue eyes (more art-
fully made up now to emphasize their luminosity), narrow
nose flaring suddenly at the nostrils, feral mouth curving outward and away from her teeth. I didn't know why she
needed that phony voice.

"My voice is my voice," she said. "If you don't like it, Peter,
you know exactly what you can do."

"It doesn't sound like your voice."

"Whose voice does it sound like?"

"My cousin's."

"Which cousin?"

"The one with throat cancer."

"Peter, that's a *terrible* thing to say."

"Speak up, I can't hear you when you whisper."

"Do you realize I'm calling long distance?"

"It sounds like you're calling from a *long* long distance."

"Do you want to go to Semanee, or don't you?"

"I'll ask David."

"When?"

"I'll be seeing him tonight."

"Okay, ask him," she said, and hung up abruptly.

I met David for dinner at O'Neal's, across the street from
Lincoln Center, where he played every Wednesday night with
the Chamber Music Society. He was dressed for the performance, wearing black dinner jacket and tie, blond hair combed
sideways and casually across his forehead, shirt front studded

with the Schlumberger set I'd given him last Christmas. He
looked freshly shaved and talced, resplendent in black and
white, and he made me feel like a shabby bum, even though I
was wearing imported Italian pants from Bloomingdale's, and
a crew-neck sweater that had cost me forty dollars of my
father's hard-earned loot. Come to think of it, I *always* felt
shabby in David's presence.

He had stopped lifting weights immediately after The Summer of Rhoda (as Dr. Krakauer in his inverted Teutonic way
was fond of describing it), but those years of jerk-and-lift had
provided him with a trim body that required very little care
and maintenance, somewhat like a concrete lawn painted
green. I don't think he washed any more often than I did, but
he always looked so goddamn clean and neat. It was discouraging. At twenty-one, my face had finally grown into my nose,
which doesn't mean it had shriveled up and been sucked into
the nostrils to disappear entirely from sight, but only that it
had finally filled out enough to disguise what I'd always considered a fairly prominent proboscis. My acne had cleared up,
too (good steady fucking from various sources works wonders,
I am told by noted dermatologists), and I usually felt very
comfortable with my appearance, a typical example of red-
blooded young American manhood—except when I was with
David, at which times I felt like a shlump. One indication of
the solidity of our friendship was the fact that I could tolerate
his clean good looks without vomiting. If there is anything I
normally can't stand, it's somebody who's better-looking than
I am. Not to mention more talented. David, that rat, had been
a great flute player (or flutist, or flautist, or whatever) even
when he was just a kid at Music and Art. But he had gone on
from there to Juilliard, and then had landed the chamber
music gig, and was also playing here and there around the city
in various symphony and studio orchestras, making a small

fortune doing what he liked best in all the world. Me? I was breaking my ass in pre-med at N.Y.U. because do you know what I wanted to be when I grew up? A psychoanalyst like the mad butcher of Ninety-sixth, the world-renowned Dr. Krakauer.

"Where the hell is Semanee?" David asked.

"In the heart of America's vast snow country," I said.

"Is it a good area?"

"According to Sandy, it's terrific."

"Can we get rooms?"

"If we move on it right away."

"When does your Christmas vacation start?"

"On the fifteenth."

"And Sandy's?"

"The twelfth."

"I have a concert on the eighth of January," David said, "but nothing between now and then." He bit into his hamburger, nodded, and said, "I think it might be fun. What do you think?"

"I think so, too."

"Is Sandy still dating that jerk from Rutgers?"

"I don't know."

"Because like, man, if she intends bringing along excess baggage . . ."

"No, she said the three of us."

"*Just* the three of us?"

"I think so."

"Can you find out for sure? When will you be talking to her again?"

"I'll call her when I get home."

"If it's *really* just the three of us, I'd like to go," David said.

"I'll find out. By the way, she's trying a new voice this week."

"What happened to the French accent?"

"She decided it was phony. You should hear what she's got now."

"Crazy girl," David said, but he was smiling affectionately.

So there we were at Semanee Lodge at the base of Semanee Peak eight days before Christmas, watching Emmanuel Schwartz pole-vaulting across the room on his new crutches. He was wearing on his round face the somewhat sickly, apologetic, guilty smile worn by anyone who's ever had an accident on the slopes, and he was wearing on his left leg the badge of his dishonor, a cast that ran from his toes clear up to his hip. Someone had already scribbled "Poor Manny!" on it with a red marking pen, but aside from that the cast was as pristine white as the sheepish grin that curled up under Schwartz's nose, its opposite ends disappearing into apple-red cheeks.

He was, this Schwartz, a round little man all over. I supposed he was in his early thirties, moon-faced, partially balding, with sloping shoulders and a pot belly, buttocks like bowling balls, fat little hands and thick thighs (the one we could see, the one without the cast), waddling forward on his crutches, grinning his silly smile in his open red-cheeked face, a man of curves angularly hobbling across the room toward the fireplace where the three of us sat toasting our feet.

"Something, huh?" he said, by way of openers.

David seemed totally absorbed in the scientific discovery that steam was rising from his socks, and Sandy was reading Story of O in tattered paperback. The main burden of conversation fell to me.

"Yes, really something," I said.

"I wanted to thank you," Schwartz said, easing himself down into a chair opposite me, and then propping his crutches against the fireplace wall. "You're the people who went for the Ski Patrol, aren't you?"

"Yes, we are," I said.

"I wanted to thank you," Schwartz said.

"Don't mention it," I said.

"I had no right being on that trail. Much too difficult for me."

David looked up from his socks and said, "Well, a lot of the fun in skiing is the challenge."

"Oh, yes," Schwartz said.

"A man's reach should always exceed his grasp," Sandy said, without so much as glancing up. She had abandoned her Breathless Whisper the moment we arrived at Semanee, probably because it didn't carry too well across the hills and dales, and whereas her voice was low-pitched now, it was at least her normal speaking voice, thank God.

"I don't believe we've met," Schwartz said.

"I'm Sandy," she said, and smiled over the top of her book.

"David."

"Peter."

"Manny," he said, and shook hands with me, and then reached over to shake hands with David, and then tried to get to Sandy's extended hand, but his leg wouldn't permit it, so he just waggled the fingers in compromise, and she waggled her fingers back at him.

"Have you three been skiing long?" Schwartz asked.

"Sandy's been skiing since she was six," David said.

"Really? Yes, of course," Schwartz said. "You're a very good skier. I saw you on the mountain even before the accident. You're very good."

"Thank you," Sandy said, and put down her book.

"Me, I'm totally uncoordinated," Schwartz said. "I don't know why I ever got involved in this cockamamy sport. I've been skiing for five years now, and all I do is get worse. Maybe I'm lucky I broke my leg. The way I feel now, if I never see snow again for the rest of my life, it couldn't be soon enough."

"Lots of skiers feel that way after an accident," David said.

"Is that a fact?"

"Sure, but as soon as they heal, they're right out there on the slopes again."

"It has to do with machismo," Sandy said.

"Well, I don't feel I have anything to prove," Schwartz said. "The way I started skiing was my brother Morris rented a house up in Manchester, Vermont, because there was a girl he was interested in, and she was an avid ski nut. So he went up there, and the house had about two dozen rooms in it, and also seven million flies, and he asked if I wanted to come up some weekend. To keep the flies company, I guess. Once you get up there, I don't have to tell you, you feel stupid as hell being so near a mountain and not at least *trying* to ski. So I tried to ski. So here I am five years later with my leg in a cast, and me an obstetrician."

"Oh, are you a doctor?" Sandy said.

"Yes," Schwartz said, and smiled modestly. "The irony is my brother Morris married that ski nut, and she's had two babies since and neither of them go skiing any more."

"The babies?" Sandy said.

"No, no, Morris and Judy," Schwartz said, and laughed. "There's a basic injustice there, don't you think? That my brother Morris should introduce me to the sport and then go home to have babies, while I'm still single and breaking my leg in a profession where I have to deliver babies standing up." Schwartz smiled quickly at Sandy and said, "*I'm* the one standing up, not the babies."

"What'll you do now?" Sandy said.

"Who knows?" Schwartz said, and shrugged. "Sit in the park, catch up on my reading, maybe give a guest lecture or two in a wheelchair. Some of the interns they got today could *use* a few lectures on how to deliver babies, believe me."

"I'll bet it's not as simple as it looks," David said.

"Who said it's simple?"

"I said it *looks* simple. Reach in, grab the head, bite the cord, slap the kid, that's it."

"Sure, sure, as simple as that," Schwartz said, and laughed. "Did you ever have to deliver a breech baby?"

"I never had to deliver any babies at all."

"It's a lot harder than delivering groceries, I can assure you," Schwartz said, and laughed again, and suddenly I began liking him.

The day I decided to become a psychiatrist, I vowed that I would never consider myself anything more than a mechanic of the mind. It was refreshing to discover that Emmanuel Schwartz, M.D., considered himself nothing more than a mechanic of the womb, so to speak. His laughter expressed genuine modesty about his profession, and yet I was willing to bet he could deliver babies sideways, upside down, or backwards with equal ease.

"Once more unto the breach, dear friends," Sandy said, and Schwartz laughed even more heartily, and managed to knock over his crutches at the same time. David picked them up for him while Schwartz fumbled for a handkerchief in the zippered pocket of his pants, thanking David between gusts of laughter, murmuring, "Oh, dear, oh that was funny," and finally tilting his head back and spreading his handkerchief tentlike over his face to dry his eyes.

I hadn't thought Sandy's quip so outrageously comic, but then I suppose I'm accustomed to expecting nothing less than

perfection from her. Smiling now, pleased by Schwartz's reaction, she said, "Are you here alone, Dr. Schwartz?"

"Manny," he said from under the handkerchief, the cloth
puffing out as he spoke. "No, I'm here with a friend. Seymour
Foderman. *He's* a lousy skier, too," Schwartz said, and burst
out laughing again.

"*Who's* a lousy skier?" a voice behind us asked, and
Schwartz yanked the handkerchief from his face, and all four
of us turned, and there stood Schwartz's twin, or a reasonable
facsimile thereof.

"Speak of the devil," Schwartz said. "Seymour, meet David,
Sandy, and Peter. My friend the gynecologist—Dr. Seymour
Foderman."

They were, Foderman and Schwartz, most certainly the
Tweedledum and Tweedledee of the medical profession. Like
Schwartz, Foderman was round and dumpy, pear-shaped,
with the same apple-cheeked moon face and pale-blue eyes,
sloping shoulders, fat behind and meaty thighs. Wearing a
green jersey turtleneck and baggy-kneed ski pants, he put
his hand on Schwartz's shoulder, and said, "Has he been
maligning me again?" and even his voice was remarkably
similar to his friend's, high and somewhat nasal, with the un-
mistakable cadences of the native New Yorker, Bronx variety.
"I happen to be a very good skier," he said, and Schwartz said,
"Oh, an expert, without doubt," and they grinned at each
other, and I realized they were about to launch into a form
of dialogue developed over the years until it was second
nature, as symbiotic as the relationship between gynecologist
and obstetrician, two old buddies working their shtik like a
pair of standup comics—except that one of them was sitting
with his leg in a cast.

"Manny, on the other hand, is exceedingly clumsy," Foderman said.

"Seymour skis with all the agility of an arthritic," Schwartz said.

"Oh, certainly, but look who fractured his leg."

"At least I fractured it with precision."

"Yes, precisely in three places."

"If you're going to break your leg, do a good job, I always say."

"You did an excellent job," Foderman said. "I understand you'll be on crutches till the Fourth of July."

"Even longer."

"I'm sure your patients'll be happy to postpone parturition."

"Indefinitely," Schwartz said and grinned at Foderman, who grinned back. Unobserved by either of them, Sandy watched the exchange, and a thin fast smile broke on her mouth. I knew at once that her imagination had been captured by these medical twins, and that something rare and exciting would happen before we left Semanee.

I didn't know what.

Dr. Krakauer doesn't really talk with a German accent. I only do him that way when I'm relating analytic atrocity stories to Sandy and David. Nor is he monosyllabic, like some psychoanalysts; we usually engage in rather lively dialogues up there in his secret laboratory on East Ninety-sixth Street. Some of these have to do with the embarrassing fact that I was still wetting the bed when I was twelve years old. Dr. Krakauer attributes this to my father's affinity for booze, his theory being that my nocturnal irrigation was a form of revenge expressed in liquid terms, the punishment fitting the crime, so to speak. But most of our conversations have to do with Rhoda.

KR: The nightmare seems definitely related. I should

imagine you'd see the relationship for yourself by this time.

ME: It's too simple.

KR: Who says it has to be complicated?

ME: I don't need an analyst to point out the obvious.

KR: If it were really so obvious, you wouldn't continue to dream about it.

ME: Dreaming about it keeps me off the streets.

KR: Nor would you make bad jokes about it.

ME: At forty dollars an hour, I can make all the bad jokes I want. Do you know the one about the man who comes to an analyst's office and starts brushing imaginary bugs off his coat?

KR: Yes, I know it. Tell me about the nightmare.

ME: I'm sick and tired of the nightmare.

KR: So am I. But until we can deal with it . . .

ME: You deal, I'll shuffle.

KR: I would like you to relate in detail the dream you had last night.

ME: It's the same dream I had Tuesday night. Don't you keep notes?

KR: Yes, I keep notes.

ME: Then take a look at them. It's the same dream.

KR: Does it start again on the Fifth Avenue bus?

ME: Yes, it starts again on the Fifth Avenue bus.

KR: And?

ME: And there's the same satchel on the seat beside me.

KR: What kind of a satchel?

ME: A black satchel.

KR: Can you describe it?

ME: A small black satchel. Like a tool box.

KR: *Is* it a tool box?

ME: No, it's a satchel. A black leather satchel.

KR: Does it remind you of anything?

ME: Yes. It reminds me of a black leather satchel.

KR: Why should it frighten you, then?

ME: I don't know.

KR: Are you frightened before you open it?

ME: Yes. I'm frightened the minute I see it.

KR: Then, why do you open it?

ME: Why does a man climb a mountain? Because it's there.

KR: Is that why you open the satchel? Because it's there?

ME: Yes. And also, there's the bus driver.

KR: What about him?

ME: He's watching me. I have the feeling that unless I open the satchel, he'll think I'm afraid to open it.

KR: But you *are* afraid to open it.

ME: I don't want the bus driver to realize that.

KR: What does he look like?

ME: His features are vague.

KR: Is he a young man?

ME: No.

KR: An older man?

ME: About your age. Eighty-nine or ninety.

KR: I'm fifty-eight. You know that.

ME: Really? You look a lot younger.

KR: Why should it matter what the bus driver thinks?

ME: He's driving the goddamn bus, isn't he?

KR: So?

ME: If I don't open the satchel, he's liable to crash into a lamppost or something.

KR: Are you afraid of *him,* or afraid of what you might find in the satchel?

ME: Both.

KR: What do you find in the satchel?

ME: Human hair.

And then we usually go into the whole boring nightmare again, which Sandy says is a farce because there's no such thing as a rape victim, and Rhoda must have *wanted* what happened to her or she wouldn't have come with us into the forest, and besides, she damn well seemed to be enjoying it while it was happening.

Monday morning, December 18, was clear and bright, but exceptionally cold. Sandy came into my room at seven-thirty, looking as though she'd deliberately dressed for the impending holiday, hugging herself and shivering in red ski underwear and a bright-green robe. I was still in bed, huddled under three blankets. The windows were covered with thick rime, and the wind outside was howling from *Nanook of the North*.

"Move over," she said, "I'm freezing," and took off the robe and crawled into bed beside me. "Don't get any ideas," she added, cuddling up against me.

"I haven't an idea in my head."

"You *are* nice and warm, though."

"Thank you. Where are we skiing today?"

"I thought the north face."

"*Today?*"

"Why not?"

"We'll freeze out there. Let's save it for a warmer day, Sandy."

"Okay, but I'm getting bored with the trails on this side." She put her arms around my waist, hugged me hard, said, "Mmmmmm," and then said, "What'd you think of Superman and Fartz?"

"Foderman and Schwartz."

"Right, right, I'm very poor on names."

"They seem like nice fellows."

"Oh, charming."

"Didn't you like them?"

"Adored them. Peas in a pod."

"They do look a lot alike, don't they?"

"Except for Schwartz's leg, they're mirror images," Sandy said, and suddenly began chuckling against my shoulder.

"What?"

"I just thought of something funny. Wouldn't it be a riot if Foderman broke *his* leg, too?"

"Oh yes, hilarious."

"The *opposite* one. Then they'd *really* be mirror images." Laughing, Sandy hugged me again, and then said, "Listen, I think I'm changing my mind."

"About what?"

"I think I'll seduce you."

"Not a chance. I'm a screaming fag. I don't dig girls."

I knew what her reaction would be, I know that girl so goddamn well. She exploded with raucous laughter, just as I'd anticipated, and then rolled herself on top of me, and straddled me, and grabbed my shoulders and began kissing me repeatedly all over my face, noisy exaggerated kisses intercut with more laughter, "A fag, huh?" and a kiss on the tip of my nose, "Yes, Sandy," solemnly, and a laugh, and a wet kiss on my left eye, which I closed just in time, "Better quit then," a loud smacking kiss on my ear, "Yes, please, Sandy, it would only become embarrassing," another kiss on my cheek, and then my chin, "No use, is it, Peter?" and more laughter, "Hopeless, Sandy."

She gave me a last wet kiss on my forehead, and then got out of bed, and put on her robe, and said, "Hurry up, Peter, it looks great out there," and went back to her room to get dressed.

I've always suspected that David *hears* life instead of seeing it. He has often compared skiing to a musical composition, wherein there is a simple statement of theme, with subsequent development and variations, and finally a restatement in full orchestral voice. Mathematically and musically, he's probably correct. There *is* an undeniable melody and rhythm to the lift line and the chair ride up, that first sugar-frosted glimpse of the summit, the soft snow-clad foothills spreading below as far as the eye can see, the choice of downhill trails, the plunge of the fall line, the force of gravity intimidating the downhill ski—a theme stated once in the morning after breakfast and developed endlessly throughout the day.

The variations are weather, visibility, and snow. Subtly or blatantly, they work on the mountain to twist the basic melody and rhythm into something unpredictable each time down—a flat white universe above the tree line, with neither sky nor shadow; a patch of glare ice around a treacherous curve; a sudden bare spot, rocks and branches jutting like tank traps out of a thin veil of snow; a drop in temperature that freezes release bindings and turns the feet aching cold inside the prison of their boots; a clawing wind that attacks the face and seeps into the goggles, the eyes suddenly wet, the trail suddenly blurred; a stretch of heavy wet powder on a runout, the skis abruptly catching, the body's forward momentum inviting disaster.

And at day's end, the restatement. The melody learned by heart, the rhythm ingrained, the danger heightened—most ski accidents occur in the waning hours of the afternoon, when weariness and lassitude combine with fading light and over-confidence (the melody learned too well, the rhythm taken for granted) to give the mountain an instant's edge, which is all it needs to splinter bones and shatter skulls.

Semanee Lodge at 4 P.M. was humming with after-concert conversation, ice in cocktail glasses clinking counterpoint. Beginners and Intermediates excitedly discussed the day's clarinet glissade ("Did you come down King's Row? God, it was sheer ice!"), expressed outrage at the oboe obbligato, condemned the ad libitum solo, and generally created a cacophonous clatter, in the midst of which (like a bored Heifetz, Cliburn, and Casals) the three of us sat by the fireplace with our feet up on the screen, socks steaming. Hans Bittner, owner of the lodge, three-time Olympics Gold Medal winner, Austrian expatriate and shmuck extraordinaire, flitted from group to group offering professional solace and advice ("Ah, yes, of course, you caught an edge") and, spotting us in serene contentment by the blazing fire, naturally decided we were unhappy and hastened to perform his hostly duties. Five feet eight and a half inches of muscle and sinew topped with an ocean of blond hair, green eyes glittering, white teeth flashing in his suntanned wolf's face, Bittner skied ski-less to the fireplace, and brought his heels together like a storm trooper on an unannounced visit.

"Well then," he said, "how was your day, my friends?"

The trouble with the way Bittner talked was that he sounded exactly like my world-famous imitation of Dr. Krakauer. Which meant that every time he launched into his formal, precise, heavily accented brauhaus number, one or another of us invariably had a coughing fit.

"Yes?" he said. "It was good? It was bad?"

"It was marvelous," Sandy said.

"A little cold," I said.

"Ah, yes, a little cold," Bittner said, and David began coughing. "Maybe it will be warmer tomorrow, though. Also, we will expect some snow."

"Good," Sandy said. "There were a lot of bare patches up there."

"Ah, yes, well, heavy traffic for the holidays, you understand."

"Ah, yes," Sandy said, and David developed double pneumonia.

"That is a bad cough you have," Bittner said.

"Ah, yes," David said, coughing.

"You should wrap the throat. Tomorrow. On the slopes. Put a wrapper on the throat."

"You hear that, David?" Sandy said. "You should put a wrapper on the throat."

"Keep it covered up," Bittner said.

"He'll do that," Sandy said. "Thank you."

"You are meeting enough people?"

"Yes, plenty, thank you," I said.

"Well, then," Bittner said, "enjoy your dinner." He smiled with all his teeth, did an abrupt about-face, and walked across the room to where some enthusiastic beginners were wildly recounting the perils of the baby slope.

"You are meeting enough people?" David asked.

"Ja, ve are meeting all zorts of pipple," I said in my Dr. Krakauer voice.

The plain truth of the matter was that we didn't *need* people. We were sufficient unto ourselves. All we needed was a setting. Semanee Lodge provided that in abundance. It was, as Sandy had promised, the very model of a perfect ski lodge snuggled into the base of a mountain: stone walls, high-beamed ceilings, huge areas of glass opening on the slopes, fireplaces blazing everywhere you looked, big floppy chairs and sofas in reds, oranges, and yellows, fat cushions scattered on rug-covered floors, candles burning in red translucent holders on pegged coffee tables, several noisy bars with excellent bartenders imported from the Costa Smeralda, a sauna downstairs, an indoor swimming pool, spacious rooms (I hate small rooms when I'm clomping around in ski boots), quilts on the beds, and oh those exciting Magic Fingers machines—if you like our brochure, please write c/o Hans Bittner, and he will complete the list for you in greater detail.

Dr. Krakauer feels that I've created in the three of us a substitute family unit, with Sandy endlessly playing the mother role, and with David and me alternately playing the father figure. There may be a smidgin of truth in this. I suppose that if one had to select a *pater familias* at random, David would be a far better choice than my own dear dad, who is hell-bent on drinking himself into that great big liquor store in the sky. The saintly Crackers, however, misses the boat when he supposes this is your ordinary, everyday American tribe, eating its way across the nation at Howard Johnson stops and peeing in Mobil restrooms. Whatever else we had going for us (good looks, intelligence, wit, humor—he said modestly), we also shared an unshakable sense of loyalty one to the other, all for each, and a communication that was almost mystical. I do not ordinarily believe in gypsy ladies or fortune cookies, but there were times when the three of us could sit by a fire (as we were doing now), saying nothing to each other, and yet knowing exactly what each of us was feeling or thinking. I don't know many family units that can do that. In fact, I don't know *any* family units that can do that. In fact, and here is where Krakauer's crystal ball begins to cloud, the important thing about the relationship the three of us share is not so much that it's a *family*, but only that it's a *unit*. And I mean exactly that—a unit. Three people acting and reacting as one person.

Before we arrived on the scene, there was zilch. The moment we debuted, bowing and curtsying to the world at large, there was a single, indestructible, forever-united entity. The day we took that fishhook from a gull's throat (we never *did* name that stupid bird) many summers back, we stumbled upon a source

of energy previously unknown to mankind, scientifically la-
beled SDP in honor of the trio that had isolated it, a rare mix-
ture of earth, fire, air, and water (plus a pinch of salt), an elixir
which when quaffed by its three happy discoverers charged
them with the power of Zero Plus Three Equals One, and
caused all previously celebrated relationships to dim by comparison. Abelard and Héloïse; Aramis, Porthos, and Athos;
Hart, Schaffner, and Marx—all such gangs-in-miniature paled
to insignificance before the blazing intensity of this newly
formed city, state, nation, galaxy, universe.

We liked each other a lot.

It was Seymour Foderman who launched Operation Machismo. We take no credit for its inception.

We had enjoyed a delicious meal prepared by a chef (Bittner assured us) who had once worked at the *Lorünser* in
Zürs. Wherever he'd worked, he knew his way around Austrian
cooking the way a mugger knows his way around Central Park.
A pair of honeymooners was sitting at the table adjacent to
ours. We did not know their names, but we instantly dubbed
them Mr. and Mrs. Penn R. Trate. Mr. Trate was most certainly an IBM'er, wearing a reindeer sweater made by Stein
Eriksen's mother, and *après*-ski slacks designed for fat-assed
young executives on the move. He undoubtedly lived in New
Canaan, commuted to White Plains, and entertained thoughts
of one day displacing Tom Watson as head of the company.
He was sporting, I swear to God (the last red-blooded American extant), a crewcut and he kept fumbling across the table
for Mrs. Trate's right hand, which, together with her left, was
occupied in slicing the bratwurst. It was our contention that
Mr. and Mrs. Trate had not yet consummated their marriage.
Mrs. Trate looked terrified. A pert-nosed, brown-haired Wasp
with enormous breasts hidden under a Minnie Mouse jumper,

she toyed with the bratwurst as though it were the realization incarnate of all her phallic fantasies, while Mr. Trate clutched for her hand reassuringly. At one point, we swore we over-heard her murmuring, "Please, not while I'm eating," but that may have been an extension of our own little fantasy.

Satiated intellectually and gastronomically, we headed for one of the more intimate lounges (all leather and wood, an orange acorn fireplace with stovepipe rising to the roof) and had the good fortune to find Foderman sitting alone by the fire. He spotted us the moment we came in, signaled us to join him, and immediately asked if we would like some brandy. Mindful of the risk we were taking (his generosity might ne-cessitate a similar gesture from us in the future), we sat with him and allowed as how we might all enjoy a little Courvoisier.

Foderman without Schwartz was bagels without lox. De-prived of his conversational foil, he said nothing, watching in-stead for a waiter, like a black man trying to hail a cab on Mad-ison Avenue. It was David who decided he might as well try breaking the ice.

"Did you ski today?" he asked, a perfectly reasonable open-ing gambit, considering the fact that we were in the heart of America's vast snow country.

"Yes, I did," Foderman said. "Ahhh, here he is now." The waiter, another Austrian import, padded up and listened in-tently, head cocked, as Foderman ordered the cognacs. Then he smiled in perfect imitation of Bittner, and went back to the bar. A heavy silence descended, threatening to smother the fire in the acorn.

"Where'd you ski?" I asked.

"Oh, all around," Foderman said.

"Enjoy yourself?" David asked.

"No," Foderman said. "It's no fun skiing alone."

"On the contrary," Sandy said. "There are only two things a person can enjoy doing alone. And one of them is skiing."

"What's the other one?" David asked, and grinned.

"Reading, smart-ass."

"I thought you were going to say masturbation," Foderman said, and blinked.

We looked at each other.

Foderman cleared his throat.

"Well," David said.

There was another silence, lengthier than the last.

"It's a shame Dr. Schwartz broke his leg," Sandy said.

"You said it," Foderman said.

"Have you skied together before?" I asked.

"Oh, all the time."

"Where do you go?"

"Vermont, mostly. We belong to a ski club. We get on a bus at Fordham Road in the Bronx, and it takes us right up to Manchester. Drinks on the bus and everything. We go almost every weekend."

"Are you married?" Sandy asked.

"Manny and me? No, we're just good friends," Foderman said, and smiled at his own little joke. He sobered immediately and said, "We're both bachelors. Neither of us has found the right girl yet."

"How old are you?" David asked.

"Thirty-five. There's still hope, huh?"

"Do you *want* to get married?" Sandy asked.

"Is that a proposal? If so, it's the nicest one I've had all day," Foderman said, and smiled again. The waiter arrived at that moment, and put the cognac snifters on the table. Foderman passed them around like an old man doling sweet wine to his children's children. Rolling her glass between her palms, Sandy said, "Are you a good skier, Dr. Foderman?"

"Seymour, *please*. Yes, I'm very good, if I say so myself."

"How would you classify yourself?"

"Advanced Intermediate."

"I see."

"I'm not an expert, you understand. But I've been skiing for a long time now, and I can handle myself. Advanced Intermediate is what I am. I can come down any trail on the mountain. In control."

"That's very good," Sandy said.

"Drink, drink, you'll wear out the glass," Foderman said, and raised his snifter. "L'chayim."

"L'chayim," Sandy said.

"L'chayim," David said.

"L'chayim," I said, and shrugged.

We all drank.

"Where did *you* people ski today?" Foderman asked.

"What were the names of the trails, David?"

"Foxglove, King's Row . . ."

"Hoarfrost, Sunglade . . ."

"I came down those trails," Foderman said. "They were very interesting. King's Row was a bit icy, but I don't mind ice. I used to ice skate a lot when I was a kid on Bronx Park East. Manny says I like skiing on ice better than snow."

None of us said a word. To a good skier, ice, snow, rocks, grass, and broken glass are all one and the same. You ski them. Seymour Foderman was a professed Advanced Intermediate, a definition suspect in itself, similar to a garbage man calling himself a Sanitation Engineer. It was Sandy who decided to get off this boring conversational tack.

"Are you from the Bronx, Dr. Foderman?" she asked.

"Seymour. Yes. Born and raised there. Right now I live on Mosholu Parkway. Near DeWitt Clinton High School. Do you know it?"

"Where's your office?" David asked.

"In Manhattan. Eighty-first and Park. Do *you* people like skiing on ice?"

There is no discouraging amateurs. I looked at Sandy, and Sandy looked at David, and David looked at me.

"Ice is nice," David said.

"I like ice," Sandy said.

"I like ice with a little scotch and soda," I said.

"A very good skier I know," Foderman said, marching in where angels, "told me that the only thing you have to remember about ice is not to try to turn on it. Just ride it out, he said. Keep the skis flat, don't try to edge, just ride it out." We were all staring at him now. "That's what this very good skier told me."

"He's probably right," David said.

"Has that been your experience?" Foderman asked.

"You should do one of two things if you hit a patch of ice," Sandy said, leaning forward.

"Yes?" Foderman said.

"You should either keep the skis flat, don't try to edge, just ride it out . . ."

"Yes, that's what this man told me."

"Or else you should dig your edges in hard and make your turn."

"Oh. He said *not* to turn."

"Well, that's up to you," Sandy said.

"The choice is yours, you see," David said.

"I suppose it's a matter of choice," Foderman said.

"Exactly," I said.

"It *would* seem better, though, to just ride it out."

"Mmm," Sandy said.

"Not that I'm afraid of ice," Foderman said.

"If you fall on ice," David said, "it's harder than if you fall on snow."

"Especially if you land on your head," I said.

"My uncle landed on his head once," Sandy said.

"Skiing?" David asked.

"No."

"What, then?" Foderman asked.

"We never found out," Sandy said. "The accident deprived him of the power of speech."

"That's a pity," Foderman said. "He probably injured something in the interior hemisphere. That's what controls speech."

"Yes, probably," Sandy said.

"My aunt got kicked by a horse once," I said.

"In the head?" David asked.

"No," I said.

"Where, then?" Foderman asked.

"In Central Park," I said.

Foderman laughed and said, "You three are regular cards. I'll tell you the truth, I wouldn't mind skiing with you tomorrow."

I hadn't recalled any of us extending an invitation, but it seemed Foderman had accepted it nonetheless. Before we could protest, he immediately said, "What time do you usually go out?"

"Early," Sandy said.

"Very early," David said. "We have an early breakfast, and off we go."

"So do I," Foderman said. "I like to beat the lift lines."

"We thought we might try the north face tomorrow," I said, hoping to put the fear of God into him.

"I've been dying to try the north face," Foderman said.

"Mostly expert trails over there," David said.

"I can come down any trail on the mountain. I came down

the Nosedive at Mansfield. You think there's anything here
I'm afraid of?"

"We wouldn't want you to break your leg, Dr. Foderman,"
Sandy said.

"Seymour," he said. "Don't worry, I'm not going to break any
leg." He paused, smiled, and then said, "Okay? Shall we try it?"

Sandy studied him for several moments. Then she returned
his smile and said, "Sure, Seymour. Let's try it."

It was raining on Tuesday morning, and so we were spared
the ordeal of leading Foderman down the treacherous (or so
we had heard) north face. I had spent another restless night
tossing and turning with The Rape of Rhoda, as Dr. Krakauer
calls it, he being wrong on two counts: the dream is *not* about
Rhoda, and Rhoda wasn't raped. I think I've read just about
every piece of literature available on rape, and rape victims,
and the psychology of the rapist, and the attitude of the police
toward rape, and if what happened in that forest five years ago
was rape, then I am Jack the Ripper and David is Bluebeard. I
keep telling that to the Ninety-sixth Street Sage, but he never
listens. I sometimes think he sits behind me and knits. Once,
I think I caught him taking a quick five-minute nap.

ME: Sandy and David both agree. I mean, we haven't
gone into a goddamn reconstruction of it, word for
word and action for action, but we certainly talk
about it every now and then, and it seems perfectly
clear to us that no one *did* anything to Rhoda she
didn't want done. She shouldn't have been drinking
beer, to begin with, she never could drink, and she
said she hated the stuff, so why the hell was she drinking it? And she wasn't crippled, you know. Nothing
prevented her from getting up and walking out of the
woods on her own two feet, if that was what she

wanted to do. So why did she stay? Sandy says it's because she smelled what was coming, and was excited by it, and maybe even *provoked* what happened, incited us to, you know, do what we did. I mean, we were all as innocent as she was, none of us had had any appreciable sex experience. That's a very excitable age, you know. I was just sixteen that summer, you know. I don't suppose *you* were ever sixteen, but you may have read Aichhorn on adolescence and gotten a secondhand impression of what it's like to be young.

KR: (Silence)

ME: *Have* you read Aichhorn?

KR: (Silence)

ME: Dr. Krakauer?

KR: Yes?

ME: Have you?

KR: Certainly.

ME: Certainly what?

KR: Certainly, I have.

Sly old fox. Forty dollars an hour, and he sits behind me with his knitting, napping while I natter. Never did admit he'd been catching forty winks, which at those rates was a dollar a wink. Well, maybe he hadn't been sleeping at all, maybe he'd been pulling the old Mute Analyst gag. But if he *had* been sleeping, it was his own fault. He was the one who insisted we go over the rape (or whatever it was) ad nauseum, as if it had been the trauma of my life, instead of just a normal adolescent experience, a loss of innocence, so to speak. I was as bored with it as he was, but *I* didn't sleep on his couch, and I didn't expect *him* to doze off while I was backtracking at his request. If Rhoda lost her innocence that summer, it was time she had. For everything there's a season, man. A time to be born, and a time to die. A time to plant, and a time to pluck up what is planted. Rhoda had been planted well and deep. (Sandy's a girl, and she ought to know what a girl feels and thinks, and *she* says Rhoda enjoyed it.) So there was Krakauer, trying his best to pluck up what had been planted, and snoring away on my time besides. It burns me up every time I think about it.

There are some skiers who will ski in any kind of weather. Hailstones can be coming down out of the sky, pots and pans can be falling on their heads, never you mind. Down the mountain they come with moronic grins on their faces, braving the elements, telling themselves they're having a gay old time out there getting hit in the face with all kinds of shmutz. Sandy, David and I may have been sex-crazed rapists, but we were not insane enough to go up on that mountain during the monsoon season. Cognizant of the fact that the snow might all be washed away by dusk, we prayed briefly (but devoutly) for a blizzard-inducing drop in temperature, and then called for a taxi and prepared to spend the rest of the day in town.

Town.

Visualize (if you must) a one-street metropolis set into the crotch of two sloping hills. Conjure a haphazard collection of boxlike buildings made of cinderblock and concrete, the flaking wooden trim uniformly painted green. On one end of town was the local garage, with a yellow tow truck backed in against a high wall of snow and a mechanic in grease-stained coveralls standing just inside the open overhead doors, staring out at the rain. At the other end of town was the diner: aluminum sides and rain-snaked windows, a white 1964 Cadillac parked below an orange neon sign that sputtered INER. Between these, a dozen stores and shops were strung out along the main drag, their windows dressed with holiday tinsel and crap—MERRY CHRISTMAS in red and green on a sagging string, SEASON'S GREET-INGS with the tops of cardboard letters mounded with cardboard snow, the bottoms dripping with cardboard icicles. Real icicles hung from copper drains as green as the town's unanimous trim; real snow was banked along the sidewalks, rapidly turning to slush, caked with soot from a train that chugged along a siding behind the stores, the tracks angling away and disappearing into the mountains. Mean-looking men in Stetsons, jeans, and boots walked silently through the pouring rain, their hands in their pockets, their heads ducked low. That was town.

We went through it in five minutes, dodging from doorway to doorway. Standing on the corner of Forty-second and Broadway, we peered out glumly at the rain.

"Well, what do you want to do now, Marty?" Sandy asked.

"I don't know," I said. "What do you want to do?"

"Gee, I don't know," David said. "What do *you* want to do?"

"How about some Christmas shopping?"

"What's today?"

"The nineteenth."

"Six more shopping days left."

"What would you like for Christmas, Peter?"

"Peace on earth."

"Be realistic."

"A Mercedes 280-SL."

"What color?"

"*I* was going to get him one," David said. "Now you spoiled the surprise."

"I'd like a new parka," Sandy said.

"What's the matter with the one you're wearing?"

"I didn't say I *needed* a new parka, I merely said I'd *like* one."

"Shall we shop around?"

"With such a wide selection of boutiques, we'd be foolish not to."

Sandy has always maintained, and I believe she's right, that you should never steal anything if you really need it or want it. Dr. Krakauer thinks Sandy is a psychopath. *I* think Dr. Krakauer is a nut. (He has never, by the way, dared to call *me* a psychopath, because that's the day I'll walk off into the sunset, thereby causing the abrupt termination of the Dr. Conrad Krakauer Endowment Fund.) The only time I ever stole anything was when I was in the sixth grade at Ethical Culture. The thing I stole was Mrs. Kingsley's hairbrush. I don't remember what I did with it.

Sandy stole quite often. I have been with her in Saks or Bonwit's when she's ripped off some really impressive items without blinking an eyelash, and each time I was so excited I nearly wet my pants. As we walked up the main street of this bustling cosmopolitan center, rain pelting us, silent cowboys striding leanly past, I found myself growing an erection of enormous proportions, and I knew it had only to do with anticipation of the caper Sandy was about to pull. David, walking on the other side of Sandy, looked extremely thoughtful and a little nervous. I wondered suddenly what the violinist, violist, and cellist in his quartet would say if they knew their flute player was at this very moment about to become an accomplice in a spectacular heist. I began to giggle.

"Shut up, Peter," Sandy said.

The crime of the century, as it evolved, was brilliant and daring. Sandy's earlier escapades had all been variations on the hit-and-run technique; you don't mess around with store detectives in Bloomingdale's or Bergdorf's. But I sensed (and it turned out that I was correct) that in a one-horse town like this, simply stuffing a parka into her bloomers would be tantamount to taking candy from a baby. Sandy had to do this job with Dash and Swagger (those well-known tap dancers) or not at all. She was wearing a blue woolen hat soaked with rain, and her blue parka was similarly drenched. Blue jeans and a blue turtleneck completed her outfit. The impression was one of total blueness, and it must have occurred to her that a quick look would convey this same impression whether she was wearing her parka or not. The first thing she had to do (and I doped this out as the Great Parka Robbery unfolded, second-guessing her along the way) was get rid of her own parka before we arrived at the scene of the crime. The department store she'd chosen to honor was midway between the garage and the diner, and she searched now for a suitable spot to dump the wet blue parka, finally coming upon an alley alongside a package store. The alley was narrow and dank, a water spout sloshing away near a collection of garbage cans and empty whiskey cartons. Taking off her parka, Sandy folded it neatly, packed it inside the top carton in a stack of four, and gently closed the cardboard flaps over it. Stripped for action, she moved swiftly through the rain, David and I following, toward the department store up the street.

The store was larger on the inside than it had appeared from out front. Two long open counters, flanking a center aisle, ran the length of the building to the shoe department at the rear. A dozen or so shoppers wandered between and around these counters, picking over the merchandise, a dazzling display of jeans, shirts, underwear, socks, buttons, sweaters, ties, and sundries. The aisle on the left, near the cash register, was equipped with a rack holding women's skirts, slacks, and dresses, men's suits, pants, and sports jackets. Along the left-hand wall was a rack loaded with overcoats, topcoats, car coats, mackinaws and (lo and behold!) ski parkas. Sandy walked directly to that rack, immediately found the parkas in her size, picked out a blue one and took it off its hanger. She tore off the sales tags, stuffed them into the pocket of her jeans, and then put on the parka and zipped it up. Taking the wet woolen hat from her head,

she wiped it over the front and shoulders of the parka to give
it at least a slightly wet look. Then, putting on the hat again,
she walked immediately toward the cash register and said,
"May I see a salesman, please?"

It was not until she reached the other side of the room that
I realized the entire operation had been witnessed by a girl
standing at the end of the aisle.

The girl looked very much like Rhoda.

She was *not* Rhoda, of course, not unless Rhoda had dyed
her hair red since that summer five years ago. But she was
about Rhoda's size, with the same chunky figure in green ski
pants and parka, the same freckle-spattered face, the same
somehow middle-aged stance, though she could not have
been older than twenty-two or -three. Our eyes met across the
long length of the aisle. She said nothing. It was too late to
warn Sandy. Her plan was in motion, and if this girl decided to
blow the whistle, there was nothing we could do about it. I
nudged David. He looked up from his nervous examination of
a black parka on the rack, saw the girl standing there motion-
less, staring at us, and immediately turned his back to her.
Sandy was returning with a salesman, blithely rattling on about
a darling parka she'd seen on the rack, which she was certain
would match perfectly a pair of bell-bottomed ski pants she'd
bought in New York. The salesman, a tall, loping cowboy-type
wearing a gray flannel suit, a string tie, brown high-topped
boots, and a prissy mustache, asked Sandy if she had the pants
with her, and she said no, but she was pretty sure of the color,
all she was worried about was the size, and into the valley of
death rode the six hundred.

Eyes prying through the portages of the head like brass cannons, so to speak, the girl in green watched with a tight little
smile on her mouth, hands on her hips—Christ, if she didn't
look like Rhoda. Unaware of her presence, totally oblivious to

the artillery across the straits there, the gun muzzles lowering
to zero in on the range and bearing, Sandy pointed out the
parka she liked while David and I hunched our shoulders and
drew in our heads, expecting an imminent explosion. The
salesman took a slick yellow parka from the rack, commented
that it was the new Wet Look, and then said, "Would you take
off your *own* parka, please?" Sandy's *own* parka, of course, was
the one she'd swiped from the rack not five minutes before,
such was the daring of her scheme. I certainly appreciated her
sang-froid and panache, but I was afraid my admiration would
not be shared by the green-garbed minion of law and order
watching from the end of the aisle as Phase II of the heist
went into effect. David's lip was beginning to tremble; his
embouchure would never be the same again. Sandy took off
the stolen blue parka (Would the salesman notice that her
turtleneck was wet after our run through the rain?) and
handed it to me. I glanced toward the girl in green. She was
still there.

Putting on the yellow parka, Sandy asked, "What size is it?"

"That's a small, miss."

"I think I need a medium," she said.

"Oh no, it fits you beautifully," the salesman said. "Don't
you think it fits her beautifully?" he asked me.

"No," I said. "It's a little tight."

"That's what I thought," Sandy said, and unzipped the parka.
"Would you have it in the next size?"

"Not in that color, no."

"That's the color I need," Sandy said. "To match the pants."

"I really *do* think it fits you," the salesman said.

"No, it's a little tight," Sandy answered, taking it off and
handing it back to him. She removed the blue parka from my
hands, noticed for the first time the panic-stricken look on my

face, smiled graciously at the salesman, and said, "Thank you very much."

"Try us again," the salesman said.

Sandy was zipping up the blue parka. She was facing the end of the aisle at which stood the green sentinel of justice, and she must have seen the girl, but her face revealed nothing. "Thank you," she said again to the salesman, and the three of us started for the front door.

Behind us, I heard the girl in green say, "Sir?"

My step quickened. Sandy, sensing something was in the wind, or probably in the air over our heads already, not realizing the something was a 155-mm howitzer shell about to explode in flying pieces of shrapnel, began walking more swiftly. We had reached the door when the girl in green said, "Do you have this in my size, sir?"

In the town's sole saloon, where we'd gone to call for a taxi after picking up Sandy's old parka, we drank beer and wondered aloud why the girl hadn't ratted.

"Maybe she didn't see anything," Sandy said.

"She *saw*," David said.

"No question about it."

"Then why didn't she tell the salesman?"

"Maybe she didn't want to get involved."

"That's the trouble with the world today," Sandy said. "Nobody wants to get involved."

"She reminded me of Rhoda," I said.

"Everybody reminds him of Rhoda," David said. "My aunt from Milwaukee, who's six feet four inches tall and a basketball center, reminded him of Rhoda."

"I have never had the pleasure of meeting your aunt from Milwaukee," I said.

"Aunt Marian?"

"Never."

"She's seventy-two years old. The minute you set eyes on her, you said she reminded you of Rhoda."

"He has a Rhoda complex," Sandy said.

"Well, this girl very definitely looked like Rhoda."

"She had red hair," David said. "Rhoda's hair was black."

"Anyway, Rhoda's in Europe," Sandy said.

"How do you know?" I asked, surprised.

"I met her."

"Where?" David said.

"In Doubleday's on Fifty-seventh."

"When was this?" I said.

"Oh, I don't know, a few months ago. She was leaving for Europe."

"How'd she look?"

"About the same."

"Did she say anything?"

"Yes, she said she was leaving for Europe."

"Where in Europe?"

"Paris, I think. Or Rome. Or London. I really didn't pay too much attention. Rhoda always bored the hell out of me."

"Did she say anything about . . . you know."

"About what?"

"That summer."

"No."

"Did she seem embarrassed?"

"Why should she?"

"I don't know," I said, and shrugged.

"She seemed fine," Sandy said. "She was looking for a French-English dictionary. Paris, it must've been."

"Why was she going to Paris?"

"I didn't ask."

"Weren't you curious?"

"Nope."

"I can just see Rhoda in Paris," David said.

"Did she ask about us? About David? And me?"

"Nope."

"Well, what the hell *did* you talk about?"

"We met in the back of the store, where they've got all the paperbacks. She said, 'Hello, Sandy,' and I didn't recognize her at first because she was wearing glasses . . ."

"Has she still got those braces on her teeth?" David asked.

"No," Sandy said. "When I realized who it was, I said, 'Hello, Rhoda, how are you?' and she said she was fine and that she was looking for a French-English dictionary because she was leaving for Paris at the end of the month. And I said, 'Paris, how exciting!' and she said, 'Yes.' Then I said, 'Well, I've got to run, it was nice seeing you,' and she said, 'Good-by, Sandy,' and that was the end of the meeting."

"I wonder why she was going to Paris," I said.

"Didn't she want to be a writer?" Sandy asked.

"She wrote for the school newspaper," I said. *"Feelings.* That was the name of her column."

"That girl in the store," David said. "You don't think she told the salesman *after* we left, do you?"

"I doubt it. He'd have come out yelling bloody murder."

"She sure seemed interested in what was going on."

"She probably thought it was a movie," Sandy said.

"What do you mean?"

"Lots of people see something happening, and they think it's a movie. They eat their popcorn, and go home afterwards, and forget all about it. It wasn't real, it was just a movie."

"That's nonsense," David said.

"I know what she means," I said. "I sometimes feel that way myself."

"About what?"

"Well . . . life. Things that happen. They don't seem real."

"Good thing you've got a shrink, man," David said, and laughed.

"You the people who called for a cab?" the bartender yelled.

"Yes," Sandy said. "Is it here?"

"Outside now."

"Thank you."

We paid for the beer and went out to the waiting taxi. The rain had stopped, and there were snow flurries in the air.

"Ladies and gentlemen," Hans Bittner said into the microphone, "I am pleased to announce that the forecast is for ten inches of fresh powder before morning."

A cheer went up from the assembled guests. We were sitting in the downstairs lounge, a room furnished in pseudo-Arlberg, with cookie-cutter shutters at the windows, orange-and-green curtains printed with little girls in dirndls and peasant blouses, wide-planked oak tables, and a trio of daytime ski instructors doubling as nighttime musicians and wearing lederhosen. The combo sat beaming in suntanned splendor behind Bittner at the microphone, pleased as kirsch that snow was falling and would continue to fall till morning. Ski instructors without snow are as worthless as last year's calendar, but these three respectively (if not respectably) played accordion, violin, and drums, insurance of a sort against washouts or droughts. They never would have made it at the old Fillmore East, or even at the Bitter End, but here in the heart of America's vast snow country, they were able to get away with their oom-pah-pah gemütlich crap since people will always applaud a trained seal playing "My Country 'Tis of Thee," not because he's a horn virtuoso but only because he's a seal. In any case, Volkmar, Max, and Helmut (for such were the gentlemen's names) sat grinning on the bandstand behind Bittner, instruments at the ready, as he concluded his announcement, and launched into an introduction.

"You have all seen our lehrers coming down the mountain, and you have no doubt noticed," Bittner said, "that they are not too bad on their skis, eh?" Bittner paused after this choice bit of litotes, anticipating the modest grins of his instructors and the appreciative nods of his audience. "What some of you may not know, however, is that they are all accomplished musicians . . ."

"Oh my, yes," David murmured.

". . . who are ready now in celebration of the marvelous snowfall to play for your entertainment and the relaxation of your muscles in dancing so you will be ready for the challenge of the mountain in the morning."

"Period," Sandy said.

"New paragraph," I said.

"So," Bittner said, "without further encouragement, I am happy to put you now in the talented hands of Volkmar, Max, and Helmut, which you will find as dependable as how they are on the slopes with skis on their feet."

Bittner grinned, moved the microphone closer to Volkmar and Max, who rose now with accordion and violin while Helmut behind them began beating out the tempo on his bass drum. As if on cue in the ballroom scene of a movie about Old Vienna, with Strauss sitting at the piano and a man in livery and white wig tapping his stick on the floor and announcing, "Their noble presences, the Duke and Duchess of Austerlitz," Mr. and Mrs. Penn R. Trate appeared at the top of the steps leading down to the lounge, she in long blue-and-white Pucci silk, hair piled on top of her head, he sporting a red velvet smoking jacket, black trousers and black patent-leather Gucci slippers. Descending into the lounge with an air of bewilderment hardly suited to their standing in the court, they passed

our table with a brief nod, and allowed one of the waitresses
to seat them near the wall. The waitress was a sweet little
townie named Alice, with whom I had been conducting a running flirtation since we'd arrived at Semanee. She was wearing
dirndl and peasant blouse to match the wee tots on the curtains, but she filled the garments much more realistically. The
band was playing something *très* Austrian. It was going to be
a fun night.

We sat through perhaps a half hour of tunes known only to
those fortunate enough to have been born in Kitzbühel, inter-
spersed with rousing old American favorites like "Roll Out
the Barrel" and "By the Light of the Silvery Moon." David
listened intently to the trio, apparently gauging their ability,
and then abruptly rose and left the table. Sandy and I both
assumed he was going outside to vomit. He returned some
ten minutes later, carrying in his hand an instrument he played
as well as the flute, an alto recorder, which came apart in three
sections and was easily packed in suitcase or coat pocket.
Without saying a word to either of us, he brushed a strand of
hair off his forehead and walked toward the corner of the
room, where the trio was cowering in anticipation of an attack from the restless crowd.

I have always admired David's sense of self, and it is no-
where more in evidence than when he is about to perform.
Completely secure in his musicianship, he comes out onto a
stage the way Muhammad Ali steps into a ring, imparting to an
audience the certain knowledge that someone is going to get
knocked cold. The very way he held the recorder, his arm dangling loosely, his fingers in a relaxed grip somewhere below
the neck, immediately communicated to the assembled guests
that he was a professional. The instrument seemed an extension of his arm and hand; he held it with such intimate
familiarity that one automatically assumed he could play it in

his sleep. The trio looked up fearfully as he approached; was
he the forerunner of the mob reprisal they were expecting?
David climbed onto the bandstand, smiled pleasantly, and
then shook hands with each of them in turn. The Austrians
now looked puzzled. He held a brief conference with them
while they listened intently, nodding all the while, and then
he smiled again, approached the microphone, and silently beat
off a fast four/four tempo with his left hand.

From the moment they began playing, there was no doubt
that David was about to metamorphose this shambling street
band into some semblance of a musical unit. He had obviously
given them the chart (all that Teutonic nodding was acknowl-
edgment that they knew and could play the chord pattern
he was laying down) and then had established the tempo, and
now he launched into a definitive demonstration of what the
recorder can sound like in the hands of an expert with a
rhythmic and harmonic background behind him. In the
ensuing twelve-and-a-half minutes of inspired jazz, David and
those Austrian shlumps sounded as if they'd been rehearsing
together for months. The three lehrers seemed shocked by
their new-found ability, and kept looking at each other in fear
and ecstasy, like snow bunnies who suddenly discover their
skis are actually running parallel. David, oblivious to everything but the beat and the chords behind him, unaware of
the crowd out front, leaned into the microphone with his eyes
shut and blew that fucking wooden horn into a silence as
deep and as reverent as a nun's fantasy.

With each new intricate lick, he led the audience down a
garden path, and then pulled the trellis down around its ears,
shattering whatever preconceived musical cliché it had anticipated. Each time he teased a melody that seemed historically
familiar, like the outcome of World War II, he so transmogri-
fied it that we were forced to accept the Japanese as victors.

His tone was as volatile as his melodic line. He shrilled notes that sounded like the second coming of the birds, whispered them like the words of spent lovers, dove deep to the bottom of the sea in a fat round bell, soared high into the stratosphere where the air was thin and you flew at your own peril. Fingers moving over the open holes in the instrument, lightly covering, tapping, lifting, covering, each note clean and sharp and true, he brought the improvisation to a frenzied climax, and then abruptly signaled the band to stop with a swift downward jerk of the recorder, bringing the audience back to its senses as sharply as if he'd snapped his fingers.

Startled for an instant, shocked by the absence of a sound they'd have followed even unto the mouth of a cannon, the guests burst into belated applause and would not let him leave the microphone until he began another number.

David was a star, and the night had finally taken off.

Dancing with Sandy, listening to David, I felt certain that the two people I loved most in the entire world had quietly conspired to make my life serene and complete. The sound of the amplified recorder, liquid and lyrical, flooded the ersatz Austrian room, while Sandy, in yellow blouse and long quilted skirt patterned with miniscule daisies, floated in my arms, her cheek against mine, her golden hair dusting my hand.

"What do you think of our friend?" I asked.

"I always knew he'd make it," Sandy said.

"Yes, but did you think he'd make it this big?"

"This is only the beginning," she said. "He'll play the Palace one day, that boy."

"Right now, he's playing only for us," I said.

"I know."

"Schwartz is watching you."

"Mm."

"So is Foderman."

"Goodie."

"Did he ask about the north face again?"

"I haven't talked to him."

"Maybe he forgot all about it."

"Not a chance."

"I think the violinist has eyes for David."

"How do you know?" Sandy said, and craned her neck for a look.

"He keeps batting his lashes."

"Maybe he's got a nervous tic."

"My dog had a nervous tick once. Kept jumping all over him and biting him everyplace."

"What's the violinist's name?" Sandy asked.

"Volkswagen?"

"Volkmar, shmuck. And that's the accordion player."

"Must be Max, then."

"Max is on drums."

"Helmut's on drums."

"Who's on first?"

"What's David playing now?"

"Left field."

"Seriously."

"Listen, dolling, they're playing our song."

"Come on, Sandy, what is it?"

"How do I know? Ask David."

"I can't. He's playing."

"What's he playing?"

"Hard to get, I think. Look at that old devil Max flirting over the bridge of his fiddle."

"If he diddles like he fiddles," Sandy said, "David's in for a rough time."

"David can take care of himself."

"I'm sure he can. He once played for a ballet company, didn't he?"

"Here comes Foderman," I said.

"What? Where?"

"Heading this way. I do believe he's going to cut in."

"Don't you dare let him!"

"Chivalry, my pet."

"Chivalry, my *ass*."

"Probably wants to ask about the north face."

"He can ask later. Don't you let him cut in, you hear me?"

"I hear you, sweet talker."

"Don't desert me."

Foderman's hand fell gently on my shoulder. "May I?" he asked.

"Why, of course, Seymour," I said, and stepped away graciously.

"Good evening, Seymour," Sandy said, and moved into Foderman's arms, and threw me a stiletto over his shoulder.

I had, I swear to Allah, no ulterior motive in abandoning Sandy to the gynecologist from Mosholu Parkway. I merely enjoyed throwing her off the roof every now and then because it gave me so much pleasure to see her land catlike on her feet each and every time. But now, as I walked away from the dance floor, I noticed Alice the waitress standing at the bar and listening to Schwartz (who sat on a leatherette stool with his left leg propped up on a hassock) and was reminded again of my eagerness to sample the viands in her famous restaurant, word of which had been ballyhooed far and wide by the ski-meisters and busboys here at Semanee. Black-haired and blue-eyed, nineteen or thereabouts, with exuberant breasts and a restless behind, she was obviously itching to dance in her dirndl to the captivating rhythms of David and the Three Shleppers. Why, then, was she wasting precious moments listening to Schwartz lecture about his fascinating fracture, his forefinger conducting a guided tour along points of interest on the now entirely scribbled-over cast? I decided to liberate her.

"Say, Manny," I said, ambling over, "I haven't signed your cast yet."

"That's right, you haven't," he said.

"May I borrow your pen, Alice?"

"Hello, Peter," she said, and batted her lashes at me the way Max the violinist was batting his at David. She unclipped a ball-point pen from the scooped throat of the blouse where it had been snuggled warm and deep, and I accepted it gratefully.

"Well, now," I said. "Let me see."

"Make it something funny," Alice said.

"Would you like something funny?" I asked Schwartz.

"Why not?" he said. "We could use a little humor in this farchadat world."

"How about 'I love Alice. Signed, Peter.'?"

"That's funny?" Schwartz asked, and shrugged.

"It's nice," Alice said, and smiled.

"I'll think of something while we dance," I said. "Be right back, Manny."

"Take your time," he said. "I'm not going anywhere."

"Better tuck this back in there," I said, handing Alice the pen.

"You can hold onto it," she said.

"Which one?"

"Fresh," she said, and smiled again, and I thought, Ah yes, we are moving into that rarefied atmosphere where intellectuals flit on gossamer wings and wit is batted about like a badminton bird.

Bittner didn't like my dancing with his waitress. He was sitting with the Trates, telling them all about the pleasures of skiing deep powder, grinning as we glided by, and suddenly the grin dropped from his face. Gaping, blinking, he silently debated whether rebuking an employee was tantamount to rebuking a guest, weighed in the positive value of my best friend having finally brought this mortuary to life, and apparently decided a dancing waitress was better than nobody dancing at all. Delighted by his good business sense, I pulled Alice a little closer.

The movie started along about then.

It was exactly what David, Sandy, and I had been discussing in the bar that afternoon. About things not seeming real sometimes. About everything suddenly looking and feeling like a movie. I don't understand it completely. I don't understand, for example, why whenever I go to a play, even though there are real people on the stage, moving in a real set with real furniture, I always know they're actors, a small part of my mind always reminds me that it's all make-believe. But when I'm in a movie theater watching the filmed images of people who are forty-seven times bigger than I am, they somehow get reduced to proper scale and the whole thing (it's only film, it's only celluloid) takes on a dimension closer to reality than either a stage play or real life. That's the part that gets me. That a film should seem more real than life itself.

The opposite of that phenomenon was exactly what began happening the moment I pulled Alice in against me. The reality started going by too fast, things began happening on the periphery of my vision and my consciousness, so that actual happenings seemed projected on multiple screens in a new technique that enabled me to be a part of the action without really being a part of it, a simultaneous observer and participant, a voyeur spying on himself over closed-circuit television in a locked closet.

I once read a book by a writer whose name I forget, where he had one of his characters lapse into third-person present whenever he thought about himself, and always in terms of a movie in which he was the star. After I finished the book, I realized why the author had done that. He had the hero talking in first-person past throughout the book (except during those movie fantasies), but he had him *die* at the end of the book, you see, and a man who's dead can't be writing about himself in the first person, past or otherwise. The writer used this film technique at the end, so that his hero could step out of and away from himself (and also out of the first-person narrative) while he was getting killed. It sounds very complicated, but it was no less complicated than what I was feeling at that very moment in time and space—that I was in a film and watching it at the same time.

Dr. Krakauer has suggested that this is not unusual in my generation, which was brought up on visual images. Sitting glued to the boob tube, we watched the products of other men's imaginations, and maybe, just maybe, thought we were exercising our own imaginations, and maybe, just maybe, thought we were a part of what was happening on the screen. Maybe that screen, because it was in the familiar environment of our own living room or playroom, became real to us—as real as the cooking smells coming from the kitchen. Dr. Krakauer holds forth at great length on topics that interest him (I suspect he's an inveterate movie buff), but he rarely clarifies for me feelings that are puzzling and sometimes, to tell the truth, quite frightening. As I danced around the room with Alice's breasts pressed hard and soft against me and my right hand sliding down toward her buttocks, I think I was a little frightened by the movie snippets flashing on those multiple screens everywhere around me. It was like losing control. I hate to lose control.

Max, the expert Austrian skier and amateur violinist, is apparently inspired by David's tootling, moves closer to him at

the microphone, and in response to his just-completed lick, un-
leashes a violin response that is not half bad. David, as startled
by the outburst as he might be if his toy poodle began reciting
Chaucer, picks up on the string solo, and tries to encourage a
musical dialogue reminiscent of those great old trumpet duels
between Elman and James. Were Max a better musician, the
result might be electrifying, recorder and violin bouncing ideas
off each other, nourishing each other, hand-in-glove, so to
speak. Max being what he is, however, the result is more like
tongue-in-cheek, even though he plays as if possessed of a
musical demon, frantically fingering, bowing, plucking, and
echoing David's intricate work.

David seems grateful to be bouncing his music off anything
at all, even Max, who is only slightly less dense than a brick
wall. He keeps encouraging Max with little appreciative nods
of the head and little beckoning dips of the recorder in his
hands. Max reaches the climax of his career when the audience
bursts into sudden applause. He almost collapses in tears,
bows from the waist, grins sheepishly, and stands by sweating
as David polishes off the one-sided duel with a wildly extrav-
agant cadenza that almost brings down the roof. Max bursts
into laughter. David laughs with him, and then they hug each
other cheerily, like a pair of Russian wrestlers who have just
thrown six Chinese out of the ring and into third row center.
Assuming undisputed leadership of the band, David signals for
Volkmar and Helmut to continue playing (wonderful little
musical aggravation you've got there, David) while he and
Max wander over to the bar to celebrate the success of their
debut.

"Oh, I'm sorry they're not playing any more," Alice said.
"Well, the other fellows are playing," I said.
"Yes, but they're not as good."
"Who needs music anyway?" I said.

"Mmm, hey, uh, listen," she said.

"Mmm?"

"I *work* here, you know."

"That's right."

"So, uh, like, take it easy, okay?"

"What time do you quit?"

"Why?"

"Thought we'd take a little moonlight stroll."

"There isn't any moon," Alice reminded me. "It's snowing."

Snow moves past the windows in silent spirals on another screen, flickering in the illumination of spotlights on each corner of the lodge. There is an inverted sense of outside being inside, as though those lighted panes of glass, stretching from floor to ceiling, with their flashing swirling broken ribbons of snow form the outer walls of another building, the room within and beyond bright with streaking white, while we, Alice and I, are outside watching. There is life in that house. I long to be inside that house where snowflakes dance.

Daisy petals flutter by, Sandy's quilted skirt flaring out from her long legs as she and Foderman waltz past to Helmut's pounding three/four beat. On the accordion, Volkmar is playing something I know, a song I heard when I was a child, but which I cannot place. I hear Sandy say, "Oh, Seymour, how you dance!" and he laughs and whirls her away, and I still cannot remember the song, though Volkmar is playing it again from the top, something, something. I swing Alice around and we oom-pah across the floor, close to the table where the Trates are listening intently to something Bittner is telling them.

We are tight on their faces, the screen here has exploded in close-up. There is a frightened expectant look in Mrs. Trate's eyes, as though Bittner is about to tell her something she is already determined not to believe. Penn Trate sits at crewcut

attention, every bristle on his close-cropped skull alert and listening, eyes drilling Bittner's face. There are state secrets being exchanged here, Bittner is telling them that the prime
minister is at this very moment being held prisoner in the
cellar. Beads of sweat stand out on Bittner's forehead, rivulets
of sweat run down his finely chiseled cheeks and into the collar of his turtleneck shirt. His eyes brighten. He pauses, says
something effectively concise, and Trate bursts into laughter.
Mrs. Trate flushes a bright crimson, and Bittner slaps the table
and throws back his head in appreciation of his own dirty joke.
In very tight close-up, Trate's hand closes on his wife's in
promise. I dance by with Alice and press against her, and wonder what is happening in that brightly lighted other room
hung with glowing white streamers.

They are sitting at the bar, David and Max. They have ordered steins of beer, and they clink the glasses together now,
and Max slurps the foam from the top of his glass, and puts his
arm around David, and laughs again. Alice is fitfully rubbing
her breasts against me. Mr. and Mrs. Trate rise from the table,
where Bittner is still laughing, and come out onto the floor and
begin waltzing delicately and beautifully. I am oddly touched
by their unexpected grace. I feel somehow they should be
dancing not here in this room to this melody from childhood I
cannot remember, but there instead in that brilliant room beyond. Sandy and Foderman have moved to a distant corner,
the screens are multiplying geometrically, my field of vision,
my conscious grasp is fragmenting into a thousand splinters.

Dizzily we waltz while Alice insistently tells me she works
here, I'd better take it easy, her breasts exploding against me
like midnight suns. Foderman has his hand on Sandy's knee,
she covers his hand with her own exactly the way Trate covered his wife's hand not two minutes ago on another screen.
At the bar, David and Max have ordered two more steins and

again Max slurps the foam off, dipping his tongue into it, and
Sandy laughs in bright contralto from across the room while
the Trates dance by and Alice moves in with her crotch and
the music stops and the movie ends.

The nightmare begins only later.

I close the satchel as soon as I realize there is human hair in
it. The hair is black and thick, it seems alive, it seems ready
to leap out of the bag at me. I snap the bag shut and look at
the bus driver, who is laughing. I rise and pull the cord, and
walk swiftly to the back of the bus. Everybody on the bus is
laughing now. I get off and stand on the sidewalk.

The city is empty.

I am the only person alive in the city.

It is very windy, and scraps of paper are blowing along the
streets. I walk for miles and do not see a single soul. The wind
is very loud, and when I call out to see if anyone else is alive,
my voice cannot be heard over the wind.

I am walking in Central Park. There is a girl sitting on
a bench, unbuttoning her blouse and licking her lips. She is
wearing bright red lipstick. She seems retarded. She keeps licking her lips and unbuttoning her blouse, opening it finally over
tremendous white breasts. The tips of her breasts are painted
with red lipstick, like her mouth. She opens her legs, and I can
see thick black hair under her skirt. I try not to look.

A man appears suddenly on the bench beside her. He whispers something to her in a foreign tongue. The girl begins
laughing. The man lifts her skirt. I try to move away, but I am
frozen to the path. I try not to watch what they are doing, but
it is impossible to turn my head or lower my eyes. The girl is
still laughing, her head thrown back. The lipstick on her
breasts has smeared, and she looks as if she is bleeding. I am
sure she is in pain, but she continues to laugh.

That is the nightmare.

A person's dreams never seem frightening to anyone but himself.

We were eating breakfast at eight o'clock that Wednesday morning in a small sun-drenched room off the main lounge, the mountain outside dressed in pristine bridal raiments, posing like a virgin before the sky above and behind, stretched as taut as a photographer's blue seamless. We always ate a good breakfast because sometimes we skied right through lunch. Sandy, especially, ate like a truck driver. Slender, fine-boned, delicate, sometimes even fragile-looking, she could put away four eggs and a dozen sausages with ease, meanwhile devouring six slices of buttered toast and drinking a half-gallon of coffee. Her concentration while eating was stupefying. She did not speak, she did not look up from her plate, she became a polished chrome piece of machinery, ball-bearinged elbow working arm and hand to shovel food into grinding mouth, phenomenal. Hunched over her plate in white sweater and blue jeans, stolen blue parka draped over the back of her chair, she worked busily at demolishing the remnants of her meal, reaching and grabbing and chewing like Henry the Eighth, and didn't even notice Foderman when he approached the table.

"Well, well," Foderman said, "good morning to you all."

David, smoking a cigarette, looked somewhat fatigued after his night of revelry with the ski-meister cum violinist. "Good morning," he said briefly.

"Ready for the north face?" Foderman asked, and pulled out a chair and sat opposite Sandy, who merely grunted and reached for another piece of toast. "How are you this morning, Sandy?"

"Fine," Sandy said, chewing.

"That was some very nice playing you did last night, David."

"Thank you."

"I enjoyed myself enormously."

David nodded.

"I've already had breakfast and seen to Manny's needs," Foderman said. "He's getting a little crotchety, talking about going home already."

"Can't blame him," I said.

"Well, I'll tell you," Foderman said, "I really *need* this vacation. If Manny goes back East, I may just stay on."

"How long had you planned to stay?"

"Till New Year's. What's today's date?"

"The twentieth."

"That gives us another what? Ten, eleven days? I can use them, believe me."

"There," Sandy said, and shoved away her plate, and stretched her long legs under the table, her buckle boots colliding with Foderman's. "Have you got another cigarette?" she asked David.

"Help yourself," he said.

"Help yourself to cancer," Foderman said.

Sandy dismissed the comment with a small tolerant shrug, shook a cigarette from the package, and lighted it.

"I have a patient this very minute dying of terminal cancer at Montefiore Hospital," Foderman said.

"Please, I just finished eating," Sandy said.

"It's not a joke," Foderman said. "You can get killed a lot easier with what you're holding in your hand there, than coming down the worst trails on this mountain."

"I've *come* down the worst trails on this mountain, and I'm still alive," Sandy said, and exhaled a stream of smoke.

"That's exactly my point," Foderman said. "Smoking is a lot more dangerous than skiing."

"Besides," David said drily, "you *haven't* come down the worst trails yet. The worst trails are on the north face." He looked at Foderman meaningfully, perhaps hoping to see him turn pale with fright.

"Take my advice, Sandy," Foderman said.

"Satan, get thee behind me," Sandy said.

"Sure, sure, it's a big joke," Foderman said, and shook his head. "You should have to visit her every day of the week. You'd change your mind about smoking, darling, believe me."

"All right, all right," Sandy said, and stubbed out her cigarette.

"Good girl," Foderman said.

Both David and I looked at her in surprise. We were not accustomed to such acquiescence.

"What'll you give up next?" David asked. "Booze?"

"Pot?" I said.

"Screwing?" David said, and Foderman blushed.

"Who's for the slopes?" Sandy asked, rising.

"We've been waiting for you," David said.

"Okay, so here I am. Peter?" she said, and then turned to Foderman. "Seymour?"

"Anytime you're ready," he said.

"Anytime you're ready, C.B.," I said, but Foderman didn't know the joke. The whole *thing* was getting to be a joke. None of us knew whether Foderman could ski fresh powder, and here we were accepting *his* invitation to accompany *us* on the north face. I kept waiting for Sandy, or David, or *somebody* (maybe even me) to say, "Look. Seymour. Buddy. The north face is pretty hairy and maybe we ought to try it on a day when we won't be up to our hips in powder, farshtein, Seymour? It's a different technique, Seymour. Let's wait till the trails are packed a bit, okay?" But no one said a word (not even me) and we clomped out of the breakfast room and down to the ski room, where we buckled our boots and put on our parkas and picked up our skis and poles and then went outside.

God, it was gorgeous.

I felt as if I were walking into that room I'd seen through the windows last night. There was no wind at all. The air was still, the mountain was hushed except for the distant sound of lift mechanisms, and far away on the access road the jingle of snow chains on a solitary automobile. We walked in silence, the four of us, skis angled onto our shoulders, poles dangling. At the base of the T-bar servicing the baby slope, we dropped our skis, dusted off the bindings, scraped thick caked snow from the bottoms of our boots with the baskets of our poles, and then stepped into the skis.

"Seymour," Sandy said, "let's take a few runs to warm up, okay? Before we try the north face?"

Foderman, crouched over his skis, fastening the safety straps around his ankles, said, "What you're really saying is you want to see how I ski before we go over there. Am I right?"

"Don't try to put anything past old Seymour," David said. "Am I right?"

"We're only concerned for your safety," Sandy said.

"Have you ever skied powder?" David asked bluntly.

"Powder shmowder," Foderman said. "I'm an Advanced Intermediate."

"Mm," David said, and blew his nose.

"Well," Sandy said, "there *is* a difference, Seymour. Since the trails on this side of the mountain'll be packed before they get to the ones on the north face, why don't we plan on spending the morning here? Okay?"

"You're the leader," Foderman said, and stood upright, and put on his mittens, and clapped his hands together.

The first thing he did was fall off the T-bar.

A T-bar, as I once tried to explain to Dr. Krakauer, is one of
the machine-powered devices used to lift skiers to the top of a
slope. T-bars, J-bars, and Pomas all *pull* a skier up the mountain. A chair *carries* him up. (If he is not careful, a *basket* carries him down.) The J-bar looks like a J, with the upright stem
attached to a strong narrow wire in turn attached to an overhead cable supported by spaced stanchions and running over
greased wheels. You lean against (but do not sit upon) the
short tail of the J, with your skis flat on the ground in a packed
snow track, and the machine literally pulls you up the mountain. A T-bar is similar to a J-bar, except that it is designed to
accommodate *two* skiers, who lean side by side against the
crosspiece of the inverted T, and are likewise pulled up the
mountain while they chat about snow conditions and temperature and how long the lift lines are. A Poma is a flat metal
disc attached to a strong narrow wire, et cetera, et cetera, et
cetera. Like the J-bar, it is designed to pull just a single skier,
the difference being that you lean against a Poma by putting
the metal disc between your legs and up against the crack of
your behind. If you are not careful getting on or off a Poma
lift, it can carry away your family jewels, provided you have
any.

In giving my brief lecture to Dr. Krakauer, I explained that
the T-bar, J-bar, and Poma lifts have always seemed to me the
most dangerous in any ski area, despite the fact that they usually service novice slopes. Chair lifts are much easier to use
(although they seem to strike terror into the hearts of beginners), and gondolas are the easiest of all, but these generally
go only to the highest reaches of the mountain. Now Foderman, anxious to prove that I was after all the seer of the uphill
ascent, promptly fell off the T-bar. He was riding up with
Sandy, and he almost pulled her down with him, but she managed to keep her balance, and then yelled back at Foderman

to get out of the track since David and I were coming up on
the bar immediately behind and were faced now with the
choice of running into Foderman or jumping off into the deep
snow on either side of the lift. Foderman, lying athwart the
track in a hopeless tangle of poles and skis, glanced anxiously
over his shoulder as David and I approached. We were midway between the loading station and the top, so the chances
of an attendant stopping the lift by pressing his emergency
button were totally nil. Inexorably, like old age, we crept up
on Foderman while Sandy kept shouting for him to crawl out
of the track. Foderman was not about to do any crawl-
ing. Panic-stricken, goggles askew, woolen hat precariously
perched like a yarmulke on the back of his head, one ski in the
air, the other twisted behind him, the straps of both poles
looped over his right wrist, he looked back at us so plaintively
that we'd have been something more heinous than puppy-dog
murderers had we not immediately abandoned ship and
dumped ourselves into the snow. Which, of course, we did,
David to the right of the track, I to the left. The bar behind
him now cleared of immediate danger, Foderman sighed in
relief and then came to the startling realization that yet another pair of skiers was approaching on the next bar, and another pair on the bar behind him, and so on ad infinitum.
Faced now with impending disaster on the scale of the
Titanic, with women and children jumping over the side
everywhere, Foderman recognized he had better get himself
out of the way fast. Scrambling, clawing, flailing to the accompanied dulcet cries of the approaching skiers, he finally rolled
out of the track not an instant too soon.

"Hello there, Seymour," David called.

"Hello, David," Foderman called back sheepishly.

He spent the next five minutes getting back into his left ski,
which had released when he scrambled out of the track. David

and I waited patiently, and then skied to the bottom with him. Sandy had gone to the top, had skied down, and was waiting for us.

"Seymour," she said, "that was ridiculous."

"I know," he said.

"Seymour, if you can't ride a T-bar, how do you expect to ski the north face?"

"I know," he said.

"Seymour, you must never do that again."

"I know, I know," he said.

He did not do it again.

We rode the T-bar to the top of the novice hill (no accidents this time) and then skied over an almost flat connecting link to the double-chair that serviced a hill marked with a blue square. At most ski areas, the trails are marked either with a green circle (for "Easiest"), a blue square (for "More Difficult"), or a black diamond (for "Most Difficult"). The three of us had skied this "blue square" hill before, though, and it was impossible to consider it "more difficult" than anything but a parking lot. Wide and gently sloping, free of moguls, covered with good packed snow, I could not conceive of anyone in the world having trouble with it—rank beginner, paralytic grandfather, or even Foderman. He and I examined the terrain below as we rode up in the chair together, at which time he told me that his first instructor had been a man who favored the Throw-the-Baby-in-the-Water approach. Equipped with a repertoire of nothing more than snowplow turns, Foderman had been taken to the top of a mountain while still a novice, had been pointed down the fall line, and told to find his way to the bottom, hit or miss, kill or be killed. That first trip down must have been a hair-raiser for everyone on the slopes. The wonder of it all was that Foderman had not crashed through the base lodge and continued on south to New York via all of Vermont, part of Massachusetts, and a corner of Connecticut. But he had, he insisted, learned a great deal from the experience. He realized on that day that he was not afraid of the mountain and that he could come down anything it had to offer. He then went on to apologize for having fallen off the T-bar, claiming such a thing had never happened to him before in all the time he'd been skiing. I assured him we all had our little mishaps every now and then, bad starts invariably led to good skiing the rest of the day, we were blessed with sunshine and lovely snow (sounding more and more like a preacher), it would only be a short while before we were warmed up enough for our assault on the north face.

"Oh, sure," Foderman said.

Sandy and David were waiting at the top.

Foderman and I skied off the chair, and then walked over to them. You can tell a lot about a skier by the way he *walks* in his skis, and Sandy was watching Foderman very carefully as we approached. His recent tumble off the T-bar had been something less than encouraging, and she must have been entertaining second thoughts along about now (as I most certainly was) on the advisability of taking Foderman along. We went through the usual skiers' ritual of blowing noses and zipping up pockets and adjusting clothing, and then Sandy asked, "Have you been down here yet, Seymour?"

"Oh yes, all the trails here," Foderman said. "They're very easy."

"Mm," David said.

Foderman lifted the goggles away from his face, defogging them, and then said, "I've been down from the *top* on this side, you know."

"Well, before we go to the top," David said, "let's take a few runs here, okay?"

"I don't normally fall off T-bars, you know," Foderman said, and smiled. "In fact, I was just telling Peter that's the first time it ever happened to me in my life."

"Mm," David said.

"Well, let's go," Sandy said, and poled in, and took off.

David followed her without hesitation. Foderman glanced at me inquiringly, and I nodded to him. This was to be the first real glimpse I'd had of Foderman in action. A pole clutched tightly in either hand, knees bent, skis parallel but wide apart, he planted himself solidly, looked straight down the mountain, and, without using his poles to shove off, leaned forward on his skis until he began a downhill plunge. Plunge it was, make no mistake. I watched in awe as he went straight down the fall line, never changing position, never traversing, never turning. Foderman was the kind of skier I normally dread and avoid. Foderman was a tank.

Schwartz, of course, on that day he'd crashed into the forest had been something of a tank himself, but nothing compared to the juggernaut that was Foderman. Foderman gaveth not a damn for man nor beast. Foderman was Patton's Third Army knocking over trees and houses, pushing aside boulders, splashing into rivers, squashing the countryside flat. Squat, burly, built low to the ground, poles as rigid as mounted cannons, boots as wide apart as fixed caterpillar treads, nothing but a Molotov cocktail (and perhaps not even that) could have stopped Foderman the Fearless on his headlong descent. To the vast amazement of Sandy and David, who were skiing close together, carving beautiful linked turns across the mountain and certainly not expecting an avalanche, Foderman went speeding past like an iron statue assembled by a junkman, and then executed a screeching stop that tore up half the hillside. Grinning from ear to ear, he lifted his goggles onto his hat, raised one pole, and signaled for David and Sandy to hurry up and join him. I had still not started down the mountain. It took me another ten seconds to recover. Still shaking my head, I shoved off.

The three of them were in conference on the side of the trail when I finally caught up.

". . . the way I always do it," Foderman was saying.

"Yes, Seymour," Sandy said, "but there are trails that won't allow such daring."

"Daring, my ass," David said. "Recklessness, you mean."

"I've never had an accident in all the time I've been skiing," Foderman said, offended. "I can stop on a dime."

"Seymour," Sandy said.

"If you don't want me to ski with you, say so."

"That's not what I'm saying."

"Then what *are* you saying?"

"She's saying you ski like a goddamn idiot, Seymour."

"Quiet, David."

"Sure, *I'll* be quiet!" David said, shouting. "Let him ski however the hell he wants to. Let him kill . . ."

"Don't you worry about me, David," Foderman said.

"You? I'm worried about *myself!*" David shouted. "Did you see him, Peter?"

"I saw him," I said. "Seymour, what you did was very dangerous."

"I'm standing here, no?" Foderman said. "I came down faster than either of them, and I'm standing here in one piece. So what's so dangerous?"

"You're a menace, that's what's so dangerous," David said. "First you force me off the T-bar, then you come down the mountain like a locomotive . . ."

"A tank," I said.

"Yeah, a tank," David said, nodding. "*Right!* A goddamn *tank!* What do you think you are, Seymour, a goddamn *tank?*"

"I'm a gynecologist," Foderman said with dignity.

"Yeah, well I'd hate like hell to have you looking up *my* cooze," David said. "Come on, let's get out of here."

"We promised Seymour we'd ski with him," Sandy said.

"Well, *you* ski with him, then. Let him hit *you* from behind!"

"I didn't hit anybody," Foderman said quietly. "I was in perfect control all the way down, and I stopped on a dime."

"Seymour," Sandy said.

"On a *dime*," Foderman said.

"Seymour," she said, "do you want to ski with us?"

"Yes," Foderman said.

"Then shut up."

On the chair ride to the top, which we were ready to assay after three runs from the midpoint, Foderman and I sat with our faces tilted to the sun, and he said without preamble, as though we had been discussing it for the past half-hour and were only continuing the conversation, "It would be easier if I could tell her."

My eyes were closed, the sun on my face was warm, the chair was moving silently on its greased cable, skiers below sent small snow-squeaking sounds into the air.

"This patient," Foderman said. "But how can I tell her? How can I say, 'Rose, you're dying'? Can I deprive her of hope? She's been my patient for eight years, she was seventeen years old when she first started coming to me. Now she's twenty-five, and she's dying of cancer, and I can't tell her. I go in every morning, and I say, 'Hello, Rose, how are you feeling today?' And I tell her what medication we're using, and I tell her there are certain symptoms we can expect, but that we're prepared for them and will cope with them, and I encourage the thought that she'll be healthy enough one day to walk out of the hospital and lead a normal, productive life. What else can

I tell her? I've tried everything. I can't save her. She's going to die, Peter."

"Well," I said, and didn't know what else to say.

"What am I, an intern?" Foderman asked. "Is this the first time I've had to look at death? Of course not! But do you know what I said to my associate? To Alan? This was just before I came out here, just before I started the vacation. I said, 'Alan, all the years I spent in medical school were a waste.' Well, what's the *sense* of all those years I spent if I can't save somebody I like? Peter, that's why I *became* a doctor, to save the people I *like*. If I can't even save the people I *like*, who *cares* about those shleppers who come in the office with a vaginal itch? Damn it, I want to save the people I like."

I turned to look at him. Foderman was shaking his head. I remained silent. It occurred to me that what passed for humorlessness in him may have been grief instead. He was mourning in advance for deaths yet to come.

"What am I supposed to tell her?" he asked. " 'Rose, you're dying'? Is that what I'm supposed to tell her? There's an Arab saying, Peter. I have no respect for Arabs, but there's a saying they have. '*Show them the death, and they will accept the fever.*' Arabs don't know their backsides from medicine, but they *do* know evil, and that's what they're talking about here— the lesser of two evils. If you show people the most horrible thing they can imagine, they're willing to settle for anything else instead. It doesn't matter *how* terrible the fever is, it can never be as awful as the death. '*Show them the death, and they will accept the fever.*' Show them starvation, they'll settle for hunger any day of the week. Show them Hitler, they'll fall in love with Attila the Hun. Without flicking an eyelash, they'll accept the fever every time because *anything's* better than the death." Foderman sighed heavily and turned his hands over in his lap, palms upward. "But can I tell Rose she's dying? Can

I say, 'Rose, you're going to *die*'? If I show her the death, if I say, 'Look, Rose, look at this hairy stinking thing coming to get you, look, Rose, I *spit* on it,' will she *then* be able to spend her remaining days in peace? *Will* she accept the fever? I don't know. I don't know what to do, Peter."

A sign on the stanchion just ahead of us informed Foderman (and indeed all skiers approaching the summit) that the thing he should do right that minute was RAISE SAFETY BAR, PREPARE TO UNLOAD, KEEP SKI TIPS UP. He had seen the sign himself. As I raised the bar, he swung his poles off the hook, and then shook his head again. We reached the platform and skied off the chair.

When I am skiing, I think of nothing but the snow and the way my body is reacting to it. Everything else leaves my head, there remains only a single-minded attention to the task of getting down the mountain in one piece. Considering the element of danger involved, I suppose such intense concentration is mandatory. I suppose, too, that this is what makes skiing such a relaxing sport. Like the snow itself, the mind becomes clean and white and empty, blank except for its occupation with the mountain. All other problems vanish.

KR: You mean to tell me you have problems?

ME: You know I have problems. That's why I'm here.

KR: I was beginning to wonder exactly *why* you're here.

ME: Well, that's why I'm here. Is this going to be one of *those* days?

KR: One of which days?

ME: Where you goad me into anger?

KR: The anger is already there.

ME: No. The anger's only there when I'm *here*.

KR: Very well. What are you angry about now?

ME: I was trying to tell you about this trip I'll be taking. I don't know why you had to twist it into something else.

KR: You said all your problems disappear when you're skiing.

ME: That's right.

KR: And I asked you what your problems were.

ME: No. You made some smart-ass sarcastic remark about not realizing I *had* any problems. And wondering why I was here.

KR: I was merely suggesting that if skiing can solve all your problems, there's no need to come here three times a week.

ME: I didn't say skiing *solved* all my problems. I said it was impossible to *think* about problems while I'm skiing.

KR: Ah, I see.

ME: You saw all along. Please cut the crap.

KR: Has it ever occurred to you that you're extremely rude to me?

ME: Never.

KR: Well, you are.

ME: Gee, I'm sorry. Would you like to lie down here beside me and neck?

KR: Would you like me to?

ME: That's a joke. I thought you knew all the analyst jokes.

KR: Yes, I know most of them. *Why* are you rude to me?

ME: Because you never understand what the hell I'm trying to say.

KR: Does *anyone* understand what you're trying to say?

ME: Yes.

KR: Who?

ME: Sandy. And David.

KR: When you tell me *they* understand you, all I get is that you understand yourself.

ME: That's not true. We're very different people.

KR: But very much alike.

ME: I should hope so.

KR: Why?

ME: We're friends.

KR: Do you have any other friends?

ME: Of course.

KR: Who?

ME: Rhoda was a friend.

KR: Yet you raped her.

ME: We did *not* rape her.

KR: Let's for the moment drop the protective pronoun, shall we?

ME: What?

KR: The "we." Let's talk about *you*. Did *you* rape Rhoda?

ME: No.

KR: Then what happened? How would you classify what happened?

ME: I don't *know* what happened. We were all good friends, I don't know what happened. We got along fine until that day.

KR: What happened on that day?

ME: We went into the forest. It was too hot on the beach, so we went into the forest.

KR: And?

ME: We started kidding around, and it led to sex.

KR: To *rape*.

ME: No.

KR: Did you force yourself upon Rhoda?

ME: We were just . . .

KR: *You*, let's talk about *you*. Did you force yourself upon
      Rhoda?

ME: Rhoda liked me a lot.

KR: You're not answering my question.

ME: I could've laid Rhoda anytime I wanted to. Why
      would I have *raped* her?

KR: I don't know why. Why did you?

ME: We didn't. Sandy was always very kind to her. We
      were all very kind to her. We taught her how to swim.
      We took her everywhere with us.

We took Foderman everywhere with us. All over the mountain. His courage was his only asset. Because of his frontal approach, his insistence upon a direct confrontation with the fall
line, we never had to wait for him to catch up; he was invariably at the bottom of any trail before we were even halfway
down. The problem was in channeling his energy. Foderman
wanted to fly, and whereas we were in sympathy with what is,
after all, one of the basic allures of skiing, we felt he should
learn to *walk* before he tried his wings so outrageously. I
honestly didn't know why we were bothering. For although I
was beginning to know him a little better, I can't say he added
any fun to the proceedings. As a matter of fact, he was a down-
right drag.

Sandy's patience with him was puzzling and a trifle annoy-
ing. She cajoled him, she scolded him, she encouraged him,
she placated him, she ignored us. At one point, she did a startling imitation of him, somewhat like an instant television re-
play, in which she fixed herself in his rigid pose and went
tearing down the mountain full tilt to execute a sudden stop
inches before she would have crashed into four startled skiers
standing by the side of the trail. "Loosen up, Seymour!" she
shouted over and over again, and Foderman would reply,

"I *am* loose!" and then squat over his skis and rumble down the mountain, God help anyone in his way. She tried to show him that skiing could be fun, that those long flat things attached to the feet could actually be *moved* at the discretion of the skier; that once they were set on a course, it wasn't necessary to assume speed and direction had been predetermined by some almighty being. "You can ski *up* the mountain, you know," she said, and he said, "*Up* the mountain?" and she said, "Sure, watch," and pointed herself at a huge boulder half-poking out of the snow, and skied down on a collision course toward it, traversing the hill. "Watch out!" Foderman yelled, and Sandy merely sidestepped the boulder by climbing in motion *up* the hillside away from it, a possibility that had never occurred to him. "Come on," she said, "let's run a little," and she began dancing up and down the hillside in a traverse, flattening the skis to slide down, and then edging to climb up, always in motion, never losing speed, gamboling like a mountain goat. Foderman could not believe such versatility was possible. He tried the exercise with clear foreboding, and then fell back upon what he knew best, a battering-ram charge on the main portal of the castle, never mind this frolicking up and down, never mind having any fun. ("Are you having any fun?" David sang, and I picked up the next line of the song immediately, "Are you getting any lovvvvving?" and we both burst out laughing while Foderman far below shrieked into his emergency stop.)

On the chair alone with Sandy, I said, "What do you think?"

"Oh, he's getting there," she said.

"It's more fun without him," I said. "I didn't come all the way out here to be a ski instructor."

"I'm enjoying it."

"Why?"

"I don't know," she said, and shrugged. "Maybe I think the

stupid bastard *will* break his leg if we don't watch over him."

"The one opposite Schwartz's."

"What?"

"You said . . ."

"Right, right. Be no fun at all if he broke the *same* leg. Which one *did* Schwartz break anyway? I forget."

"The right one, I think. Or the left."

"Sure that eliminates all the possibilities?"

"Reasonably sure."

"Try to be a bit more adventurous, Peter. Take a gamble. Right or left? I'd hate for Foderman to end up with the *wrong* broken leg."

"Well, if he breaks the right one, we're safe."

"How so?"

"How can the right one be the wrong one?"

"Wild laughter and applause," Sandy said.

"You didn't think that was funny? I thought it was very funny."

"Oh my, yes."

"At least as funny as a broken leg."

"What is your obsession with broken legs, Peter dear?"

"Mine? I was about to ask the same question."

"I have no interest whatever in broken legs. Just talking about them makes me nervous."

"Yet you were the one who raised the matter of broken legs, Sandra dear."

"I beg your pardon, *you* were the one."

"Me? I have a morbid fear of broken legs."

"I have a morbid fear of turtles," Sandy said.

"To me, a broken leg is like a broken promise," I said.

"More lusty applause, cheers from the balcony."

"You didn't think that was literary? I thought it was very literary."

"That's one of your shortcomings, Peter. Thinking." She tapped her temple with a gloved forefinger. "Nothing upstairs, Peter."

"Dr. Krakauer agrees with you."

"He does? I retract my statement."

"He says if I *thought* a bit more, I wouldn't have to act-out all the time. Acting-out is neurotic."

"I should think so. I prefer indoor performances myself."

"Sandy, dear . . . ?"

"Yes, Peter dear?"

"Do you know what acting-out is?"

"Of course I do."

"What is it?"

"You're the one who's spent four years on a couch . . ."

"*Three* years."

"And you're asking *me* what acting-out is? Go ask Dr. Crackers."

"What does he know about true love?"

"Ahh, Peter, what does *anyone* know about true love?"

"True love is a fountain."

"True love is a broken leg."

"There you go, Sandy. Back to broken legs. You know what I think?"

"There *you* go, Peter. Back to thinking."

"How else would I know I exist?"

"Try stopping on a dime."

"Thinking is safer."

"Not the way you think."

"Actually, I'm a very good thinker."

"Actually, you've got a bad lisp. Has anyone ever mentioned that to you?"

"Not until this moment."

"Think about it," Sandy said.

"Listen," I said, "let's get rid of Foderman."

"Sibling rivalry, Peter?"

"I admit it, Dr. Crackers."

"Well, let's try it a bit longer, okay?"

"We've already *tried* it a bit longer. He's a pain in the ass."

"I want to see what happens," Sandy said.

Nothing happened.

By the end of the day, I was convinced we'd done our best with Foderman, but that it was impossible to teach an old dog new tricks or even to force a horse to drink from water to which he has been led. David was equally discouraged. Only Sandy seemed to have enjoyed herself. In the ski room, when Foderman asked, "Shall we try the north face tomorrow?" Sandy cheerfully replied, "I think you're ready for it, Seymour."

David and I looked at each other sourly, and went upstairs to the bar.

I was on my third scotch and soda when Alice the waitress wandered into the bar. Sandy had gone to her room for a nap after her strenuous day of coping with Foderman the Intrepid, and David had gone downstairs to play ping-pong with Max the Meister. I felt totally abandoned, deserted, ditched, and depressed. Alice, much to my surprise, was not dressed in her customary dirndl and blouse. Instead, she was wearing tight black ski pants and a black jersey turtleneck shirt. Nipples poking and peering into the room, she spotted me where I was nursing my drink, and immediately perambulated over.

"Hi, Peter," she said.

"Hi, Alice."

"Have a good day?"

"Terrific," I said. "Where's your costume?"

"What? Oh. This is my day off."

"Did *you* ski?"

"Yep."

"Have a good day?"

"Terrific," she said, and grinned.

"Want a drink?"

"I wouldn't mind," she said, and climbed up onto the stool beside me. To the bartender, she said, "A whiskey sour, straight up, please."

"Right, Alice," he said, and winked at me.

"What was that for?" Alice whispered.

"What was what for?" I asked.

"The wink. You didn't say anything to him, did you?"

"What about?"

"Last night."

"What would I say?"

"I don't know," Alice said, and shrugged.

"All we did was dance."

"That's right."

"So what would I say?"

"Nothing."

"Okay."

"Then why did he wink at you?"

"Maybe he saw us dancing."

"He wasn't on last night."

"Maybe somebody *else* saw us dancing and told him about it."

"There's nothing wrong with dancing," Alice said.

"Who said there was?"

"Even *close* dancing."

"Of course not."

"So why did he wink?"

"I honestly don't know. Why don't you ask him?"

"Him? I wouldn't ask him the right time."

The bartender came over with the whiskey sour, put it on the bartop, smiled, and said, "Here you go, Alice."

"Thank you, Robert," she said. She waited until he had returned to the other end of the bar, and then she whispered, "If I was stranded on the Sahara without a watch, I wouldn't ask him for the right time."

"I gather you don't like him."

"You gather right," she said, and lifted her glass. "Cheers."

"Cheers," I said.

"He almost raped me once," Alice said conversationally.

"Oh, really?"

"Yeah," she said, and drank. "That animal."

"Must have been terrifying."

"Terrifying? It was disgusting."

"I'll bet it was."

"No goddamn self-control," she said, and shook her head. "It's not that I'm a virgin, you know . . ."

"No, I didn't know that."

"Well, I'm not. But there *is* a limit, you know. I mean, you expect a person to have at least a *little* self-control."

"Certainly."

"That's what I like about you."

"My self-control," I said, nodding.

"Yes," she said, and drank again. "Robert has no self-control at all."

"Well, he probably finds you very attractive."

"Oh, sure," Alice said. "Who wouldn't?"

"Nobody."

"But he practically tore off my clothes. I mean, what the hell is *that?*"

"Terrible," I said.

"Right," she said. "Could I have another one of these?"

"Sure," I said. "Robert, another round, please."

"In his grubby little room over the slaves' quarters," Alice said. "I don't even know why I went up there."

"Why did you go up there?"

"He said he wanted me to hear a new record he had."

"Pretty shabby trick."

"Shabby? You said it. Started getting crazy the minute he closed the door. He's got a hundred hands, he's not a bartender for nothing."

"Tch," I said.

"I was just so embarrassed, I didn't know what to say."

"What *did* you say?"

"What could I say? I put on my panties and left."

"I don't blame you one little bit."

"So now he winks," Alice said.

"Whiskey sour, and a scotch on the rocks," Robert said, and put down the drinks.

"Thank you," I said.

Robert nodded, glanced at Alice, and then reluctantly went back to the other end of the bar.

"Cheers," Alice said.

"Cheers," I said, and we both drank.

"Mmm, good," Alice said.

"Did you find it cold out there today?" I asked.

"Cold? No. Cold?"

"In that outfit, I mean."

"This outfit?"

"Yes. Didn't you get cold?"

"No."

"I thought you might have got a bit chilly."

"No," she said. She sipped a little more of her drink, and then said, "Oh, you mean because I'm not wearing a bra."

"Yes."

"I never wear a bra when I'm skiing."

"Neither do I."

"I like to feel free and easy when I'm skiing."

"So do I."

"A bra is a pain in the ass," Alice said.

"I'll bet it is."

"You're a nice person, Peter," she said.

"Thank you."

"I feel very free and easy with you."

"Maybe that's because you're not wearing a bra," I said.

"What?" she said, and then smiled and said, "Fresh."

"Listen," I said.

"Um?"

"Would you like to come to my room and hear a new record I have?"

Alice peered at me over the rim of her glass. Then she put the glass down on the bartop, and smiled slowly, and said, "*You* won't try to rape me, will you, Peter?"

It was like a movie.

We came into the room, and I locked the door.

"Why are you locking the door?" she asked.

"I don't want anyone to interrupt us," I said.

"All we're going to do is listen to a new record."

"I don't have a new record. I don't even have a record player."

"So what *are* we going to do?"

"Why don't we sit and talk a while?"

"We were sitting and talking in the bar, why'd we have to come up here to do the exact same thing?"

"It's more private here."

"You *are* going to rape me, aren't you, Peter?"

"Don't be silly."

"I can tell."

I offered her a drink, and she refused the first time, and then I offered her a drink again when the silence seemed to lengthen interminably, she sitting in the wingback chair near the frost-rimed windows, I perched cross-legged on the bed, and this time she accepted. I went to the dresser and carried the bottle of scotch into the bathroom and I said there was no ice, and she said she didn't care for any ice, it was very hot in the room. I put a little tap water in both scotches and then I carried them back into the room and handed her one of them, and she sipped at it, and kept watching me over the rim of the glass and she said again, "It's very hot in here, Peter."

"Well," I said, "they always keep the rooms very hot at ski lodges."

"Yes, I've noticed that."

"I guess it's because you can see all that snow and ice outside and it makes people feel better if the room is hot."

"All it does is make me feel uncomfortable, that's all."

"Well," I said, "why don't you take off that shirt?"

"Uh-uh," she said, and sipped at her drink and kept watching me over the edge of the glass. "What is this?" she asked. "Scotch?"

"Yes, it's scotch."

"I was drinking whiskey sours in the bar. Will I get sick?"

"No, you won't get sick. It doesn't matter about mixing drinks, that's a lot of crap."

"Naughty language," she said, and smiled. "It *is* hot in here, though."

"So take it off," I said.

"Uh-uh," she said. She stretched out her legs, and then kicked off her fur-lined boots, first one and then the other. "Mmm," she said, "that's better."

"It'd be even better if you took off the turtleneck," I said. "I mean, because the room's so hot and all."

"Yes, it is," she said, "but I don't think it'd be appropriate for me to sit around in just my ski pants."

"Why not?"

"Well, I wouldn't want you to get excited, Peter."

"We're good friends, Alice. I don't see anything wrong with you taking off the turtleneck since it's so hot in the goddamn room."

"Well it *is* hot," she said.

"Well, why don't you take it off, then?"

"Well, okay, but remember your promise."

"What promise?"

"Your promise not to rape me," she said, and put her glass down on the floor, and pulled the turtleneck up over her breasts, but not over her head, sat sprawled in the wingback chair with the shirt bunched up above her breasts, black against white. She picked up the glass, and I got off the bed and walked to where she was sitting with her legs outstretched, and stepped over her legs so that I was standing with my own legs apart, straddling her.

"Let me help you," I said.

"No, thanks," she said, "I'm fine this way."

I pulled the shirt up over her head, and threw it on the floor. She looked up at me, and said nothing, and put her glass down on the floor beside the chair again, and then picked up the shirt and tossed it onto the bed. She lifted the glass, still saying nothing, and sipped from it.

"That's better," I said.

"I'm glad you think it's better," she said.

I was still standing in front of the chair, staring down at her, my legs apart, her long legs stretched out between them.

"Well?" she said.

"Nice," I said. "Look at your nipples."

"I've seen them, thanks."

"Look at them anyway."

She looked down at her breasts and said, "So what?"

"Get up," I said.

"I'm fine right where I am, thanks. Get me another drink, please." She extended the glass to me, and I took it from her hand and poured more scotch into it and was starting for the bathroom when she said, "I don't need water, thanks," and I brought the glass back to her and she accepted it and said, "I don't want a scene with you like I had with Robert."

"Oh?" I said. "Did you take your shirt off for Robert?"

"Of course not, what do you think I am?"

"I seem to remember you had to put on your panties before leaving his room."

"Who told you that?"

"You did."

"No, I couldn't have put on my panties because they were ripped."

"How'd they get ripped?"

"Robert ripped them."

"Are you wearing panties now?"

"No, just ski underwear."

"What color?"

"Red."

"Why don't you let me see them?"

"No, I don't think long johns are very attractive," she said.

"I feel certain you look magnificent in long johns, especially with that sweet little ass," I said.

"Naughty language, Peter."

"Come on, take off the ski pants."

"It's too much trouble."

"I'll help you."

"Thanks, I'd rather leave them on. You'll only get excited. You won't be able to control yourself."

I was standing by the dresser and looking at her where she sat sprawled in the chair, lazily sipping at her drink, smiling at me over the glass. I moved to her, gently took the glass from her hand, and reached behind me to put it on the dresser.

"I'll *rip* them off," I said.

"You'd better not try."

"I'm warning you, Alice."

"What's so special about seeing me in my long johns?" she asked, and stood up and unzipped her ski pants at the side, and then lowered them to her knees and sat in the chair again and said, "Help me." I pulled the elastic bottoms off her feet and then tossed the pants over to the bed, alongside the black jersey shirt.

"Now stand up," I said.

"What for?"

"I want to see you."

"You can see me fine just the way I am," she said. "Give me my drink, please."

"You've had enough to drink."

"No, I haven't. Give it to me."

"Get up," I said.

"I'll get up, but only because I want my drink," she said, and rose immediately. Moving flatfooted to the dresser, resembling a healthy dancer wearing rehearsal tights, she picked up the glass of scotch, and I knocked it from her hand. She did not appear at all startled. She looked down at the glass and the spilled whiskey on the rug, and then lifted her head and said, "What a waste of good scotch," and put her hands on her hips and said, "What now?" Her eyes were mocking and challenging and bright, but her lips were trembling.

"You *know* what now," I said.

"I'm afraid I don't."

"Now you take off the underwear."

"Now I put on my clothes and get out of here," she said, and went for her pants and her shirt. I grabbed her wrist and swung her away from the bed. Still holding her wrist tightly, I forced her to her knees and with my free hand unzipped my fly.

"That doesn't scare me," she said.

"What doesn't?"

"That thing."

"What thing?"

"That."

"What do you call it?"

"Nothing."

"What do you call it?" I said.

"Nothing," she said. "It doesn't scare me."

"Then take it," I said.

There was no difference between her and Rhoda. They were identical. Willing rape victims.

Sandy was right.

Schwartz was the one who started telling doctor jokes after dinner. With his broken leg propped up on a chair (the left one, by the way, and now decorated with a scrawled endorsement from yours truly: Schwartz for President! Signed, R. Nixon) we sat around the acorn fireplace in the small lounge and Schwartz told the old chestnut about the proctologist examining the patient who'd swallowed a glass eye, rearing back (so to speak) in surprise and saying, "I've been looking up assholes for fourteen years, and this is the first time I've ever seen anyone looking back!" Everyone laughed politely, except Foderman, who was apparently hearing the joke for the first time, and who collapsed in gales of uncontrollable mirth. Thus encouraged, Schwartz told another medical story, this one about the immigrant who visits a doctor because his wife has been having so many babies, four or five in as many years, and he doesn't know how to stop her alarming reproductive rate. The doctor realizes the poor man knows nothing about contraception and explains the use of condoms to him, telling him he must absolutely put one on his organ each and every time he contemplates intercourse. Well, a month later, the immigrant comes back and tells the doctor his wife is pregnant again, and the doctor looks at him in surprise and then chastisingly says, "Did you put the condom on your organ, as I told you to do?" And the immigrant says, "I don't have no organ in the house, Doc, so I put it on the piano instead."

This one, too, convulsed Foderman, which led Sandy to throw in a quickie about the girl who comes to the doctor and says, "I haven't fenestrated in a month, and I think I'm stagnant," to which the doctor replies, "You mean you haven't menstruated in a month, and you think you're pregnant," and the girl says, "All I know is my boyfriend reached a climate and he wasn't wearing a phylactery."

David, who had heard all of these jokes around the pool hall at the Philharmonic, yawned politely and glanced over his shoulder toward the bar, where Max Brandstaetter (for such was our violinist's full name) was in deep conversation with Robert the Rapacious Barkeep. I thought David might get up and wander over for a beer and some musical discourse, but instead he said, "Do you know the one about the man who comes to a doctor with an infection of the big toe?"

"No," Schwartz said, "tell it."

"Tell it," Foderman said, grinning in anticipation, and leaning forward in his chair.

"Well, this man comes to a doctor with a bad infection of the big toe, an open sore dripping pus, terrible mess. The doctor examines him, takes some smears, and announces in surprise that the man has gonorrhea of the big toe. This is the first time in my life I've ever had a patient with gonorrhea of the big toe,' the doctor says, and asks the man's permission to report it at the next medical convention."

"I never heard of it, either," Foderman said, chuckling. "Gonorrhea of the big toe."

"Well, at the medical convention, the doctor gets up before his colleagues and says, 'I wish to report an astounding phenomenon. In June, I treated a man in my office for gonorrhea of the big toe,' at which point a doctor in the audience raises his hand and says, 'Excuse me for interrupting, but in June *I* treated a woman in my office for athlete's twat.'"

Sandy and I burst out laughing simultaneously, but Foderman and Schwartz sat in stunned silence. (Had Alice been present, she would most certainly have said, "Naughty language.") Foderman looked at Schwartz, who finally smiled. Taking his cue, Foderman also smiled, though he was blushing a bright pink.

"There must be a thousand doctor jokes," Schwartz said at last.

"A million," Foderman said, and all conversation jolted to a halt.

"Well, I think I'll have a beer," David said, and rose and walked to the bar, where Max greeted him effusively.

KR: Have you ever thought David might be homosexual?

ME: Don't be ridiculous.

KR: Is the idea repellent to you?

ME: Abhorrent.

KR: Why?

ME: Because I know he isn't.

KR: Have you ever discussed it with him?

ME: Never.

KR: Why not?

ME: Because if you know how to spell "cat," you don't
look it up in the dictionary. I *know* David isn't a fag.

KR: How do you know that?

ME: He sleeps with girls, *that's* how I know it.

KR: Might he not also sleep with boys?

ME: No, he might not also sleep with boys.

KR: If you've never discussed it with him, how do you
know?

ME: He's my best friend. He would have told me.

KR: Perhaps he knew you would find it abhorrent.

ME: I do.

KR: Yet *you've* slept with David.

ME: I've been in the same bed with him, if that's what you
mean.

KR: Yes, of course that's what I mean.

ME: And Sandy was with us.

KR: Sandy slept between you.

ME: Yes.

KR: On every occasion?

ME: On every occasion. Besides, it hasn't happened that
often.

KR: How often, would you say?

ME: Three or four times.

KR: When was the first time?

ME: Sometime after that summer.

KR: The summer of Rhoda?

ME: Jesus, I wish you'd stop calling it that. A lot of *other*
things happened that summer, too. You don't have to
label it like the Pleistocene Age or something.

KR: *Is* it that summer you're talking about?

ME: Yes, that summer.

KR: And the first time you, David, and Sandy slept in the
same bed together was shortly after that summer.

ME: In the fall sometime. November, I think.

KR: Where?

ME: At Sandy's house. Her mother was away with Snow White for the . . .

KR: Snow White, did you say?

ME: Yes, this guy she was going with at the time. I forget his real name. We used to call him Snow White.

KR: Why?

ME: Because he turned lobster red in the sun.

KR: I don't see the connection.

ME: Forget it.

KR: In any case, Sandy's mother was away with him.

ME: Yes, for the weekend. And Sandy called us up, and we stayed in the apartment with her.

KR: Was there only one bedroom in the apartment?

ME: Of course not.

KR: Then why did you all sleep in the same bed?

ME: What's the matter, doctor? Are you shocked?

KR: Hardly.

ME: It goes on all the time, you know. This is *now,* Doctor. We aren't back in the Middle Ages, you know.

KR: It went on in the Middle Ages, too, I understand.

ME: And anyway, it wasn't what you think. It wasn't sordid or . . . shocking. It wasn't shocking. I don't know why the hell you're shocked.

KR: I'm not.

ME: That's right, you get all kinds of lunatics and perverts in here, don't you?

KR: All kinds.

ME: It was, in fact, a very good experience.

KR: I see.

ME: You don't believe that, do you? Well, it was. Grown-ups have some crazy ideas about . . .

KR: Grown-ups?

ME: Yes.

KR: You're twenty-one, Peter.

ME: I know I am.

KR: That makes you a grown-up.

ME: I'm trying to say we weren't grown-ups at the *time*. This was five years ago. And it wasn't an *orgy* or anything like that, the way grown-ups always think of . . . of any arrangement that isn't quite conventional.

KR: On the contrary, there are many grown-ups who have exactly such unconventional arrangements. They are not the exclusive property of the young.

ME: I'm not talking about a *ménage à trois*, Doctor.

KR: I didn't think you were.

ME: Nor even a *folie à trois*.

KR: You've been reading.

ME: How else would I be able to follow you?

KR: In any case, you feel it was a good experience.

ME: Yes.

KR: For all three of you?

ME: Yes. Well, how do *I* know? It was good for me. I enjoyed it.

KR: You enjoyed making love to Sandy?

ME: I still do.

KR: Did David enjoy it?

ME: I never asked him.

KR: I thought you talked about everything.

ME: We didn't talk about that.

KR: Why not?

ME: It was something the three of us shared together, there was no reason to beat it to death afterwards. We did it because we wanted to do it, and we enjoyed doing it, and that was that.

KR: And apparently you enjoyed it enough to repeat the experience again and again.

ME: Three or four times. We don't make a habit of it.

KR: Why not? If it's so enjoyable . . .

ME: I don't think you understand the relationship between the three of us.

KR: Perhaps not.

ME: If we feel like going to bed together, that's what we do. There aren't any set rules, Doctor. This isn't a club.

KR: It sounds somewhat like a club.

ME: All I'm trying to say is there aren't any set rules.

KR: I can see that. If, for example, you and *David* wanted to go to bed together, there'd be no rules against that, either, would there?

ME: The matter has never come up.

KR: But if it should. I don't suppose there'd be any rules against it.

ME: David's not a fag, Doctor. Let's just get that straight. David is *not* a fag.

KR: Fine.

At some point during that tiresome evening we spent in the lounge, Schwartz announced that he was leaving in the morning; he was sick and tired of sitting around all day with nothing to do, he would be better off in New York City, where at least his brother and his wife could come over to play Monopoly with him. Foderman offered to play Monopoly with him right there at Semanee, but Schwartz said, "What fun is Monopoly with only two people? No, Seymour, I'm going home tomorrow. I've already made the airplane reservation."

A general gloom settled over the crowd. The crowd, as such, consisted solely of Seymour Foderman. Sulking like a vaudeville performer who has just been told that Ziegfeld wants

only his partner and not the act, trying bravely to maintain a
stiff upper lip in the face of Schwartz's desertion, Foderman
began talking about the north face, and about how eager he
was to try it in the morning. I think he wanted to make
Schwartz jealous. I think he was saying, "Look, Manny, who
needs you? You want to go home, go ahead. I got these nice
bright kids I can ski with, they're going to take me over to the
hardest part of the mountain, who needs a cripple like you
hanging around and complaining? Go on, go home. Go play
Monopoly with your brother and his dreary wife, who cares?"
But he was hurt.

David wandered over from the bar with Max in tow, to tell
us that the instructors were getting up a game of broomball on
the ice-skating rink, and would we care to join in? Broomball
is hockey without skates and without a puck. Instead, each
member of the team, equipped with a broom and wearing his
normal footwear, runs around the ice trying to knock a basketball into the goal. The idea is to fall on your head and break
your cranium. Sandy told David that one of her least favorite
leisure-time activities was playing broomball, and I told him
I would have been happy to join them if I hadn't just had
broomball for dinner, thank you, and off he went to slip and
slide.

"The north face," Foderman said, "is supposed to be more
difficult than Ajax." He paused significantly and said to
Schwartz, "Ajax. At Aspen."

"How do you know how bad Ajax is?" Schwartz asked.

"I heard about it. And I also heard about the north face
here."

"Who cares?" Schwartz said. "By this time tomorrow, I'll be
sitting in front of my nice fireplace, burning cannel coal and
listening to Beethoven's Fifth."

"Aren't you even curious about it?" Foderman asked.

"Certainly, I'm curious. You can tell me all about it when you get home."

"I could tell you all about it tomorrow."

"I won't be here tomorrow."

"I'm saying *if* you stayed."

"I already made a plane reservation."

"You could cancel the reservation."

"Listen to this guy, will you?" Schwartz said.

"He's concerned about you," Sandy said gently.

"Sure. He's so concerned, he runs off skiing all day long. While I sit around twiddling my thumbs."

"Manny, it isn't my fault you broke your leg," Foderman said.

"I know it isn't. Who said it was your fault?"

"I'm only suggesting," Foderman said, "that you could have a good time here even *with* the broken leg. That's all I'm suggesting, Manny."

"I could have a better time in New York."

"Doing what? Playing Monopoly?"

"And also seeing a certain person who called here today to find out how I was."

"Ah. So that's it."

Schwartz nodded.

"Well, I hope you have a good flight," Foderman said. "What time are you leaving?"

"The car is picking me up at eight."

"I'll help you with your bags," Foderman said.

"Thank you, I would appreciate it."

Foderman rose, seemed about to say something more to Schwartz, but instead turned to Sandy. "Shall we meet for breakfast?" he asked. "After I get Manny on his way?"

"If we're going over to the north face," Sandy said, "we ought to get started as soon as the lifts are running."

"Don't worry about me," Schwartz said. "I can put myself in the car."

"You've got a broken leg there," Foderman said. "How're you going to manage by yourself?"

"There are bellhops, don't worry. Have your breakfast and go try the north face."

"Are you sure?" Foderman asked.

"I'm sure, I'm sure."

"What time will you be eating, Sandy?"

"Seven. But don't expect conversation from me."

"What I *could* do," Foderman said, "is have breakfast with Manny and make sure his bags are all out front. And his skis."

"You don't have to bother," Schwartz said. "Look at him, will you? A regular Jewish mother."

"Well, we'll talk about it in the morning," Foderman said.

"There's nothing to talk about. Have a good sleep, eat your breakfast, and go ski the farshtinkener north face. I'll see you in the city."

"We'll talk about it in the morning," Foderman said again. "Good night, everybody."

"Good night already," Schwartz said.

Daybreak Thursday morning was one of the most spectacularly beautiful I'd ever been privileged to witness. Awakened early by my persistent you-know-what, I dressed and went downstairs through the silent lodge, and then ventured outdoors in those last few moments before night's candles had burnt out and jocund day stood tiptoe on the misty mountaintops. I had seen many dawns before, of course; in the city where the sun lumbers up over the rooftops like a bloodstained mugger; at the shore, where it springs out of the ocean like a Japanese dancer in silks; in the country, where it blinks like timid semaphore through the foliage and then runs molten behind the silhouetted trees. But I had never before seen it in the mountains, and I was truly stupefied.

It was a religious miracle.

I fully expected Jesus Christ to come over the summit to the accompaniment of heraldic trumpets.

Instead, a solitary skier came down the novice slope.

The skier himself (or herself, it was difficult to tell from this distance) was something of a miracle in that the lifts were not yet running, and he (or she) must have *climbed* to the top of the slope. Since dawn was just breaking, this meant that the uphill ascent had been made in near-darkness, not a difficult feat but certainly an energetic and unusual one. I automatically assumed that the skier coming down the slope was an insomniac, and I began to construct a little fantasy involving him (or her) lying in bed counting ascending chairs in a fruitless effort to drop off to sleep, finally saying the hell with it, and coming out to sidestep or herringbone to the top. It did not take much skill to come down the wide, gently angled hill, but the skier was obviously a good one, wedelning with graceful ease, wearing green parka and pants that seemed in perfect calm harmony with the sun-pink snow.

The skier was a girl.

As she came closer, intent on the slope, plunging directly down the fall line (such as it was) in short clicking beautiful tight motion, I saw red hair streaming from the sides of her green wool, tasseled hat and thought for a moment That's the girl from the department store, and then thought No, it isn't, and then she was fifty feet above me, and then thirty, and twenty, yellow goggles covering half her freckled face, ten feet, five, Yes, it was the goddamn girl who'd witnessed the theft, and she carved a quick short stop and looked up at me.

"Hey, hi," she said.

"Hi," I said.

She lifted the goggles off her face. Her eyes were the color of her parka, a lime green. "I hate to be corny," she said, "but haven't we met before?"

"No," I said, "I don't think so."

"Sure," she said. "You were shopping," she said, and winked.

"I think you're mistaking me for someone else," I said. "How's the snow?"

"Gorgeous," she said.

"Well, have a good day," I said.

"Sure," she said. "You, too."

Getting Schwartz off to the airport was a monumental operation. We had got a later start than intended, waiting forty-five minutes for breakfast because something was wrong with one of the kitchen stoves, and the chef was working at half his normal speed. By the time Sandy's flapjacks and sausages came, it was almost ten minutes to eight, and she was ready to kill. I knew exactly how she felt; breakfast is the one meal I want *when* I want it. The three of us ate ravenously, and then went outside to join Foderman and Schwartz, who were waiting for the airport car and fussing over Schwartz's luggage and skis. Schwartz was traveling with six (count 'em) *six* matched suitcases; someone had apparently told him he was spending four months in Europe. The luggage was piled against the side of the building, his boots in a black carrying case, his skis bagged and leaning against the wall. Foderman counted the luggage, and then counted it again, and said, "Six pieces, am I right, Manny?"

"Six pieces, right."

"And the skis make seven."

"Seven, right."

"And the boots. That's eight."

"Eight, yes."

"Make sure they give you eight baggage checks."

"Would you like to pin a little note to my coat?" Schwartz asked. "With my name and address on it? And who to call in an emergency?"

"I'm only worried because of your leg," Foderman said. "Whose luggage is this?"

"The other people who are going in the car."

"Where are they?"

"Paying their bill."

"Did *you* pay your bill?"

"I paid it."

"Where's the car?"

"It'll be here."

"I don't want you to miss the plane."

"I won't miss the plane."

"It wouldn't be fun sitting around an airport with a broken leg."

"The car'll be here, I won't miss the plane."

"Did you pack everything?"

"Everything."

"I'll check the room later, just to make sure. Anything you missed, I can take home for you."

"I didn't miss anything, you don't have to check the room."

"Just in case. Have you got your ticket?"

"In my pocket."

"You're sure?"

"I'm sure."

"Let me see it."

"For Christ's sake, Seymour, it's right here in my pocket!"

"Just in case."

Schwartz reached under his overcoat and into his jacket pocket and pulled out his airline ticket. "All right?" he asked.

"Put it away now," Foderman said. "Before you lose it."

The car arrived at a quarter past eight. Foderman counted the luggage again, and then supervised the loading of it. Sandy was beginning to get a bit impatient by then, anxious to ski over to the north face before the lift lines grew impossibly long. But Foderman checked the skis on the roof rack, making sure they were strapped on solidly, and then counted the luggage in the trunk again, and then said, "Your boots! Where are his boots, driver?"

"They're in the back there," the driver said. "Alongside the spare."

"I don't see them," Foderman said.

"I put them in myself," the driver said.

"Then, where are they?"

"Right there. The black bag."

"Okay," Foderman said, and nodded curtly and went around to the side of the car to help Schwartz in. Schwartz handed me one of his crutches and then leaned on Foderman's shoulder for support, and eased himself onto the seat. Foderman held the broken leg as Schwartz swung it into the automobile, and then asked, "Have you got enough room, Manny?"

"Plenty of room. There's only the three of us going."

"Where are they, anyway?" Foderman asked nervously. "They should be out here by now."

"They'll be here, don't worry."

"Listen, ah, Seymour," Sandy said, and looked at her watch.

"In a minute," Foderman said. "I want to get him settled."

"I'm settled already," Schwartz said. "My bags and boots are in the trunk, my skis are on the rack, my ticket's in my pocket, and I had a very nice bowel movement this morning. Go enjoy yourself, will you please?"

"I wanted to wait till you left," Foderman said.

"There's no need," Schwartz said. "Get him out of here, will you?"

"Come on, Seymour," Sandy said.

"Have a good flight," I said.

"Thank you."

"Take care of yourself," David said.

"Thank you, thank you. Maybe I'll see you in the city."

"Call me when you get home," Foderman said. "Call me tonight."

"Okay."

"You promise?"

"I promise."

As we walked away from the car, Foderman shook his head and said, "I wanted to wait till he left."

As it turned out, our haste to get to the other side of the mountain was entirely unnecessary. We battled the lift line to the midway station on the southern side, and then transferred to the double chair that took us to the summit. Foderman kept looking over his shoulder toward the base, as though hoping to catch a glimpse of Schwartz departing. (Foderman was beginning to get on my nerves.) From the summit, we skied over two links and four downhill trails to the base on the northern side, complicated are the ways of mountains. It was ten-thirty by the time we got there. The chair lift to the summit of the north face was not operating. There were strong winds on this side of the mountain, and the empty chairs were bouncing and bobbing with each fresh gust.

Sandy stopped a Ski Patrolman and raised hell with him, demanding to know why someone on the *other* side of the mountain hadn't informed anyone that the goddamn chair on *this* side of the mountain wasn't working. The Ski Patrolman snippily informed her that he was merely a Ski Patrolman and not responsible for the operation of lifts or announcements concerning the operation of lifts. Sandy told him to drop dead. The problem now was how to get back to the other side. We held a brief consultation with a group of other disgruntled skiers, and learned that there was a milk run around the base of the mountain (mostly walking) which would eventually lead us back.

It was one-thirty before we got around to any serious skiing. The lift lines were incredible. Because the north face was closed, all of the skiers were on the southern half of the mountain. I clocked a half-hour wait for the lower chair, and a forty-minute wait for the one to the summit. We caught a quick hamburger in the restaurant up there (imaginatively called Skytop) and then started down a narrow chute far over on the right, heading for the Poma that serviced a remote area dotted with bowls and laced with interlocking trails and a network of T-bars. It would be possible, we thought, to ski there all afternoon, from T-bar to T-bar, down a different trail each time, over difficult but uncrowded terrain.

Foderman began having trouble almost at once.

The chute would have seemed his meat and potatoes, a long straight drop angled at about forty-five degrees and opening into a wide run-out. But traffic had made the chute a bit icy, and whereas Foderman's mechanized cavalry charge might have chewed it up under normal conditions, he lost his balance shortly after he began his descent, and his right ski slipped out from under him when he tried to straighten up. He went into one of those crazy windmilling falls that are as terrifying as they look, skis, arms, legs, poles cartwheeling down the mountain in a cloud of snow, the skier helpless in the grip of gravity, his only hope being that one or both skis will release before he breaks his legs. Foderman's right ski was the first one to pop. His left boot snapped out an instant later, with such force that it tore the safety strap. The runaway ski went hurtling down the chute, hit a mogul halfway down, and took off into the air like a flung javelin. Foderman continued his rolling, bone-jarring descent, right ski flailing on its short restraining strap, banging him across the shins and arms. The other ski, the free one, the one without a rider, went sailing past Sandy, missing her by three inches and almost tearing off her head. It landed in the woods with branch-rattling force, embedding itself deep in a snowbank, quivering as if in terror itself. Foderman finally came to a stop when he hit soft snow at the bottom. Lying flat on his back spread-eagled, poles still on his wrists, the right ski loose under him, the left boot buried, his face white with fear and crusted snow, he sucked in air and waited for us to ski over to him.

"You okay?" Sandy said.

Foderman grunted.

"Hey! You okay?"

Foderman grunted again.

"I think he's hurt," David said.

Foderman shook his head.

"Get that ski from under him," Sandy said.

"We'd better pull him out of the way here," I said, and glanced anxiously toward the top of the chute.

"Loosen that strap, David."

The safety strap was fastened around Foderman's ankle with the usual push-clip, caked now with snow. David cleared the metal, snapped it open, and slid the ski out from under him.

"Let's move him," I said. "Before somebody else comes barreling down here."

"Suppose he's hurt?" David said. "You're not supposed to move . . ."

"Not hurt," Foderman mumbled.

"It speaks," Sandy said, and Foderman began laughing.

By actual count, Foderman fell twenty-seven times that

afternoon. The man was indestructible. He fell on his back, his left side and right side, the front and rear of his head, his knees, his elbows, his behind, his chest, his ear, his nose, and probably his pecker. The falling got to be a habit. I think the son of a bitch was enjoying it. We were prepared for him to fall whenever the going got rough, of course, but now that Foderman had the hang of it, he fell at every conceivable opportunity. If the terrain was flat, Foderman fell. If it was gently rolling, he fell again. He fell in deep powder, he fell on packed surfaces, every time we turned around, *bang!* there was Foderman on the ground. It might have been comical if we hadn't wasted half the day getting over to the north face and back again, and then wasted *more* time in the ski shop buying a new strap for Foderman's left ski, and were now wasting the *rest* of the day getting him on his feet and helping him into his bindings and dusting him off and wiping his nose and pointing him down the mountain toward his next tumble.

It was Sandy who, leaning over Foderman after one of his more spectacular falls, suggested that his bindings were too loose. Foderman, lying flat on his back and out of breath, said, "No," and shook his head.

"They're too loose," Sandy insisted. "That's why you're falling all the time."

"Had them adjusted this morning," Foderman said, panting.

"Well, whoever adjusted them did a lousy job."

"The ski shop adjusted them."

"Have you got a wrench, Peter?" Sandy asked.

"What are you going to do?"

"Tighten his bindings."

"The bindings are all right," Foderman said.

"Then why do you keep popping out of your skis?"

"How's this?" David asked, and pulled a short stubby screwdriver from his pocket.

"Fine," Sandy said, and accepted the screwdriver and then crouched over Foderman's skis. "I think the left one's okay," she said. "It's the right one that keeps releasing."

"They were both adjusted this morning," Foderman said, and sat up, knees bent, to watch Sandy as she brought the screwdriver to bear on the head of the binding's turnscrew. I once told Dr. Krakauer that the moment someone invented a foolproof release binding, skiing would lose much of its excitement, my theory being that the inherent possibility of fracture was what attracted so many people to the slopes. Krakauer, as usual, missed the point. A binding, I went on to explain, held the boot rigidly fastened to the ski, a shotgun-wedding essential to the translation of *leg* motion into *ski* motion. If the binding was too loose, the spring mechanism could be triggered by the slightest bump or turn, and the ski would release prematurely. If, on the other hand, the binding was too tight, there would be no release at all, even in the worst spill. Since something's got to give in a bad fall, the leg (being merely flesh, bone, and blood) has priority over most of the skis on today's market (they being constructed of plastic, metal, laminated wood, and what-have-you). There are machines that "scientifically" adjust the settings on release bindings according to the weight of the skier, and presumably these machines guarantee maximum maneuverability and safety—you come out of your bindings only when the pressure is severe enough, but not before.

Sandy did not have a machine on the mountain. All Sandy had was a screwdriver. It occurred to me (but fleetingly) that she was now adjusting only the binding on Foderman's right ski, and I recalled (but fleetingly) that we'd done a lot of joking about Foderman breaking the leg opposite Schwartz's. The right leg. Her face was intent as she twisted the screw.

"Not too tight now," Foderman said.

"Just a half turn," Sandy answered.

But she had already turned the screw a full three hundred and sixty degrees.

"Not too *tight*," I warned.

"He keeps falling out," Sandy answered. "It's more dangerous that way."

"Yes, but . . ."

"Shut up, Peter," she said, and turned the screw another full circle. "There," she said. "That ought to do it."

"I hope so," Foderman said, and clambered to his feet. He looked down at his skis, nodded, said, "Thank you," to Sandy, and then brushed off his pants.

"Straight to the bottom, okay?" Sandy said. "Last run. And no falling, Seymour."

"No falling," he promised, and grinned broadly.

He kept his promise. He did not fall again. I kept waiting for him to fall because I was certain the binding would not release. I was positive he would break his right leg. Sandy, skiing in the lead, kept glancing back over her shoulder, anticipating, I am sure, the same thing I was. But he did not fall, and when we reached the bottom I sighed in relief, I think.

In the lodge that night, Hans Bittner announced that four inches of fresh powder were expected before morning. "And that's only fitting, my friends," he said, "because this, as you know, is December twenty-one, and that's the first day of winter."

TWO

MARY MARGARET

Semanee Valley was an island.

Not too distant from that sophisticated urban center from which Sandy had stolen the parka, it was nonetheless totally removed from it in tone and style. The area had been conceived of and designed as a self-contained town, a decision undoubtedly arrived at after taking one look at the existing shamble of buildings not thirty-seven miles away. Unlike many ski areas, there was no base lodge as such, but rather a collection of tastefully executed hotels and inns clustered about the highest mountain in the range, the mother of a family of lesser hills that surrounded it. Semanee Lodge was the biggest hotel in the valley, but the others were equally well-designed and excellently managed. The planners of the valley had connected the hotels, shops, restaurants, and discotheques with a simple grid arrangement of wooden sidewalks, redwood two-by-fours spaced to swallow the falling snow, illuminated by lamps that flickered with imitation gaslight. At night, the valley looked like the opening shot of the village in Walt Disney's *Pinocchio*. During the day, its architecture snuggled harmoniously against the spectacular background of Semanee Peak and its suckling brood—wood, stone, glass, nature in realized fantasy.

The snow which had started the night before in celebration
of the winter solstice, continued into Friday morning, accompanied by the high winds that yesterday had been tumbling
the chairs on the north face. We tried a few runs down from
the midpoint on the southern side (unaccompanied by Foderman, who had *not* received the promised call from Schwartz,
and who was either sulking, pouting, or weeping) and then
decided to call it quits. It was three days before Christmas, and
none of us had as yet done any shopping.

The stores in the valley were largely oriented to skiing needs,
of course, but they offered a surprisingly large selection of
other merchandise as well, ranging all the way from artsy-
craftsy crap to hand-wrought jewelry and Indian rugs. The
better to keep our gifts secret (even the tightest triumvirate
keeps *some* secrets), the three of us split up and went our
separate ways, arranging to meet for lunch in a place that
served charcoal-broiled sirloins, baked potatoes and salad
for a dollar and ninety-five cents, cheap at half the price.

The girl in green was looking at a pewter pot in the second
shop I entered.

The bell over the door tinkled, I saw the girl, decided to
leave, realized she had already spotted me, and wondered
what I was afraid of. All right, she had seen Sandy swiping
the parka. Let her prove it. I closed the door firmly behind
me, and started directly up the aisle toward her. My dear old
mother, when she was not worrying silly about my father
crashing into a lamppost in a drunken stupor, told me again
and again that the only way to conquer the slings and arrows
of outrageous fortune was to confront them. I was ready for
that confrontation now. High noon in the heart of America's
vast snow country.

"Hello," I said, "how are you?"

The girl in green seemed surprised by my boldness. She had

undoubtedly decided that since she was the only witness to
the multimillion-dollar robbery three days earlier, we des-
peradoes would forever avoid her, would spend the rest of
our lives like Jean Valjean fleeing Javert. The initial surprise
gave way to a quick grin that cracked hard and sharp across
her face. She had nice teeth. Otherwise, she was a singularly
plain girl, with a dumpling face and frizzy red hair and freckles
spattered like specks of paprika across the bridge of her nose
and her cheeks.

"Hey, hi," she said.

"Been up there today?" I asked.

"Just one run."

"Pretty miserable."

"Ghastly," she said. Her voice was a trifle grating, rising in
inflection so that every sentence she uttered sounded like a
question. "You guys are pretty good skiers," she said.

"Thanks."

"I watched you yesterday."

"Really? We didn't notice."

"Who's the fat man?"

"A friend."

"Really? Is he Jewish?"

"What?" I said.

"Is he a Jew?" she said.

Her question, to say the least, was somewhat startling. If you
are born into a certain New York socioeconomic strata, you
don't go around asking if people are Jewish. You just don't.
You dress British, and you think Yiddish, and sometimes you
even contribute funds for the planting of trees in Israel.
Several questions of my own came immediately to mind. As,
for example: (1) How had she been able to guess, from her
distant glimpses of Foderman, that he was Jewish? (2) How
was she able to tell for certain that *I* was *not* Jewish, and there-

fore risk asking a possibly offensive question? and (3) What the hell difference did it make?

"He's a Buddhist," I said.

"He's a Jew," she answered. "Who are you kidding?"

"So?" I said.

"So?" she answered. She had a direct way of looking at a person, green eyes opened wide and unblinking. "He's going to break his leg if he isn't careful. He's in way over his depth." She paused, grinned, and said, "Or is that the idea?"

"I don't know what you mean."

"To break his leg," she said.

"I still don't know what you mean."

"I think you know what I mean," she said.

I really *didn't* know what she meant. We certainly had no intention of deliberately breaking Foderman's leg, if that's what she meant. We had made some jokes about it, sure. But fun is fun, and purposely setting out to break a person's leg (the *right* one, no less, for the joke to be effective) was something beyond our engineering skill and beneath our sensibility. Anyway, Schwartz was already gone; the joke would be lost entirely if Foderman followed east without his accompanying mirror image. And besides, all our kidding had been done in private; unless this freckle-faced fink was blessed with extrasensory perception, how had she possibly reached the ridiculous conclusion that we were skiing with Foderman in order to hurt him? The entire concept was preposterous. I decided to change the subject.

"That's a nice pot," I said.

"It's pewter," she said.

"Yes, I know."

"I admire the way you ripped off that parka," she said.

I blinked.

"Real finesse," she said. "Want to stick this under your sweater for me?"

"Stick it up your ass," I said, and walked out of the shop.

It was snowing quite heavily, and the wind was murderous. From out of the vortex of spiraling biting miniscule flakes, there materialized a hairy, three-headed, shambling monster bellowing to the wind. My encounter with the girl had shaken me more than I'd realized; my initial instinct was to turn and run from this snow beast advancing inexorably in its own white cloud, roaring what seemed at first to be a message of doom. I froze to the sidewalk in panic. The creature lumbered closer, reformed itself in a shifting crystalline miasma, nucleus spreading and tearing apart into three separate hairy cells, still advancing. Squinting through the snow, I now recognized two boys and a girl, each wearing long raccoon coats, arms wrapped about each other, shouting, "Get Semanee!" at the top of their lungs again and again, "Get Semanee! Get Semanee!", stomping past, almost knocking me off the sidewalk, and then moving off into the flying snow, merging again into a single marauding hair-covered animal, and disappearing entirely from sight as the last echo of their chant died on the wind. Immediately ahead of me now, emerging from the same dizzying tunnel that had spawned the first apparition, there appeared an amoeba-like blob threatening to swallow the valley, advancing on the sidewalk to assume discernible shapes—a half-dozen skiers bellowing, "Up Snowclad!", all of them wearing buttons that read, "Get Semanee!"

The dawn came a little late.

When we'd first arrived and bought our lift tickets, we were each given buttons bearing the legend, "There *is* no Snowclad!" We learned later that Snowclad was a fiercely competitive resort some hundred miles to the north, boasting a higher elevation and a greater average yearly snowfall. These, then, were the outraged Snowclad people, here to defend their honor, making goddamn fools of themselves by parading in a snowstorm and bleating the ridiculous words "Up Snowclad!" and "Get Semanee!" What they intended to *get* was beyond me. The valley? The mountain itself? But onward they came, more and more of them, in pairs and in threes, in dozens and droves, completely filling the wooden walks of the town, wearing their childish buttons and chanting their fanatical slogans—"Get Semanee! Up Snowclad! Get Semanee!"—while the snow kept falling and the wind kept blowing and the end of the world seemed near.

I bought Sandy an exquisite cameo brooch with a profile as delicate as her own, and for David I found a white canvas, shag-lined, Swedish Army coat with dozens of huge pockets. I carried both gifts back to the hotel, and then went over to the steak joint to meet them. Sandy was already there, drinking a Manhattan.

"The streets are full of Mongolian ponies," she said.

"I ran into them."

"Goddamn idiots," she said.

"I also ran into Miss Nemesis."

"What'd *she* want?"

"She asked me to steal a pewter pot."

"Did you tell her to flake off?"

"I did. She thinks we're trying to break Foderman's leg."

"That's ridiculous," Sandy said.

"Of course it is."

"Why would we want to break Foderman's leg?"

"Exactly."

"More goddamn crazy people in the world," Sandy said. "You know what those jackasses in the street are?"

"No, what are they?"

"Conforming nonconformists."

"Thank you, Dr. Crackers."

"Ja," Sandy said, "dot's right, don't make fun. Conforming nonconformists. You tink they are free, Peter? Ah, no. *Nein, liebchen.* Their behavior is rigidly prescribed."

KR: But why a sestina?

ME: I don't understand your question.

KR: Well, to begin with, I didn't know poetry interested you.

ME: It doesn't.

KR: Yet you wrote a poem.

ME: I was just fooling around with one, that's all.

KR: And you chose the sestina form?

ME: Yes.

KR: Well, that's my question. Why such a rigid form?

ME: I thought it would be fun. If you're going to try writing a poem, you might as well start with a challenge. Are you familiar with sestinas?

KR: I know a little about them.

ME: There are six stanzas, you see, each composed of six lines . . .

KR: Yes, I know.

ME: And the end words of the lines in the first stanza are repeated in different order in the next five stanzas. No rhymes. Just those six recurring words at the end of each line in each stanza.

KR: But in different order.

ME: Yes. Different in each stanza.

KR: And the order is a fixed one.

ME: Yes, it's predetermined. I mean, that's the form. You *have* to use the end words in the order prescribed. Otherwise you don't write a sestina. It's one, two, three, four, five, six in the first stanza, and then six, one, five, two, four, three in the next stanza, and so on.

KR: One might say the end words are repeated through-out in a fixed pattern of cruciate retrogradation.

ME: Thanks, smart-ass.

KR: I told you I knew a little about sestinas.

ME: You *seem* to know a lot about them. Aren't you going to mention the three-line envoi at the end of the poem?

KR: Why does my knowledge infuriate you?

ME: I don't like being put on, Doctor.

KR: I merely wanted to find out what your understanding of the form was.

ME: Do I pass the test? Do I understand it?

KR: You seem to understand it. Why did you pick this particularly inflexible mode of expression?

ME: I told you. It seemed like a challenge. Also, it's repeti-tive and hypnotic, and anyway, go to hell.

KR: What was the poem about?

ME: The three of us.

KR: You and Sandy and . . .

ME: Yes.

KR: Then perhaps you chose the form so you could super-impose order upon a chaotic relationship.

ME: The relationship is not chaotic.

KR: How did you come upon the form to begin with?

ME: What do you mean?

KR: The sestina.

ME: I was looking up "sex" in the dictionary.

KR: Are you putting *me* on now?

ME: No, I'm putting you *down*. There's a difference, Doctor.

"Where are you, Peter?" Sandy asked.

"Huh?"

"Did you hear anything I said?"

"All of it."

"What's bothering you? That girl?"

"I guess."

"Forget her. She can't touch us."

The girl in green arrived at Semanee Lodge shortly before dinner that night. I was coming out of the bar, and was crossing the lobby on the way to my room, when I saw her standing at the desk. There were two pieces of luggage at her feet. I felt the way I'd felt earlier, when I saw the hairy apparition through the swirling snow; I wanted to turn and run. It was too late. She had seen me.

"Hey, hi," she said.

"Hi," I said, and cautiously approached her. She was signing the register. She had luggage with her. She was checking into the goddamn hotel.

"You the welcoming committee?" she asked, and put the pen back on the registration card holder, and then smiled.

"Nope. Didn't even know you were coming."

"Neither did I," she said. "I stayed here last year, but they were booked solid when I wrote in December."

My heart was pounding. What are you afraid of? I asked myself. Nothing, I told myself. I was scared witless.

"I've been staying at the Inn," she said. "And calling here every day to see if there were any cancellations."

"I take it there was a cancellation."

"Nope. Somebody checked out unexpectedly."

"Schwartz," I said.

"What?" she said.

"Nothing."

"So here I am. Are you guys staying here?"

"Yes."

"Well, good."

"Yes, wonderful," I said.

"That's Room 207, Miss," the desk clerk said.

"Would you have someone take up the bags, please?" she answered, and turned again to me. "Why don't you buy me a drink?"

"I just had a drink."

"Have another one."

"I had another one, too."

"Are you afraid of me or something?"

"Why should I be?"

"God knows. Shall *I* buy *you* a drink?"

"That might be better."

"Why?"

"The other way sounds like blackmail."

"Blackmail? What are you talking about?"

"I think you know exactly what I'm talking about."

"The parka? Who cares about that? I'm trying to make your acquaintance, jerk."

"Why?"

"I like your style," she said, and looped her arm through mine, and grinned. "Okay?"

We studied each other. "Okay," I said, and we walked toward the bar. I was still frightened. She made me frightened.

The bartender on duty was our old friend Robert the Rapist. "Hey, hi," she said, apparently having made his acquaintance during her previous stay at the Lodge, and eager now to renew the doubtless fascinating relationship. Robert looked at her vaguely. "Mary Margaret Buono," she said.

"Oh, yeah," Robert said. "How are you, Mary Margaret?"

"Just fine, thanks."

"You're back, huh?"

"I'm back," she said. "I've got a dry-cleaning bill I've been saving for you."

"Huh?" he said.

"What are you drinking?" she asked me.

"Scotch on the rocks."

"Make it two," she said to Robert.

"Nice to see you again," Robert said, and went off to get the drinks.

"What's your name?" she asked me.

"Peter."

"Mary Margaret."

"I gathered."

"Nice to meet you."

In the next half hour of conversation, I tried to analyze why I was afraid of Mary Margaret. (This is a very good thing to do when you are away from your shrink. To begin with, it helps you to understand yourself, and at the same time it makes you feel you don't need a doctor at all. It is very beneficial. It is also difficult. It becomes even more difficult when you're trying to do it while another person is filling you in on her life and times.) Mary Margaret was a marathon talker. She was also a pretty good drinker. I stopped counting after her fifth scotch. I think I also stopped listening, so occupied was I in trying to learn why she frightened me, while simultaneously trying to keep up with her phenomenal capacity for putting away the sauce. We both got pretty drunk in that next half hour. That's the only way I can possibly explain my feet.

The first thing I considered in the analysis of my fear was her resemblance to Rhoda. But why should that have frightened me? Besides, whereas my first impression had been of a girl remarkably similar in appearance to Rhoda, closer scrutiny along the bar convinced me I had made not only a visual error, but a personality goof as well. Mary Margaret was as unlike Rhoda as two turnips in a cornfield. I rejected the Twin Sister Theory and continued to examine the nudging unconscious urge to get away from her before she somehow hurt me. In the meantime, we kept drinking scotch as though the barley supply were in imminent ecological danger.

"I'm twenty-four years old," she said, "and I've got a B.A. in education from Hunter College, which thank God I'll never have to use. I earn on the average of fifteen hundred dollars a week, most of which I sock away in the bank as insurance against the day my hands begin to wither. It's a nice feeling, believe me."

"Fifteen hundred a week," I said.

"Yes," she said.

Occupied as I was with self-analysis and drinking, I could not at the moment pay any *real* attention to Mary Margaret's peculiar problem, which at first glance appeared to be schizophrenia of the paranoid type, with accompanying delusions of grandeur. I listened nonetheless while she recited a touching Rags-to-Riches tale (Italian Immigrant variety) about herself and two brothers living in Queens with Mama and Papa in the shadow of the Triboro Bridge, Papa eking out a mean living as a cab driver, Mama employed as a file clerk with a Wall Street firm of lawyers, all of it changing the moment Mary Margaret hit it big. She was somewhat vague as to exactly *how* she'd hit it big, seeming a bit embarrassed about revealing the source of that fifteen hundred bucks a week. This led me to reconsider my earlier appraisal of Mary Margaret as blackmailer, and to analyze this concept in terms of my irrational fear.

The fact was that she *had* witnessed a crime, and that I could reasonably be considered an accomplice to that crime, having acted in concert with Sandy when she was ripping off the parka. In which case, should Mary Margaret decide to go to the police, there existed the possibility that David, Sandy, and I would be charged with larceny and spend the rest of our lives in prison, where David would become star soloist with the prison orchestra, and where I would learn firsthand how to treat the criminally insane, thereby realizing all my psychoanalytic ambitions. Sandy, meanwhile, would languish in the women's section and become a notorious lesbian. My mother would bring me chocolates and cigarettes every other Tuesday, remarking on my prison pallor and asking if the food was good. Eventually, I would be returned to society after having paid my debt, severely chastened, old and stooped, marveling at the fact that a joint Russian-American-Chinese team had landed eighteen men on Jupiter just the day before. In my boozy state, the notion seemed more amusing than frightening. If Mary Margaret ever *did* turn informer, there simply was no way to prove that Sandy had actually stolen the parka. Who was to say she hadn't bought it back in the city? Was a person supposed to save all her sales slips in the unlikely event some lunatic might one day accuse her of shoplifting? Preposterous. Then why was I frightened?

"My father used to drive only at night because there was more money in it—you know, the traffic's lighter and the tips are bigger. He got held up six times in Harlem. The last time he was sixty-four years old. He got out of the cab with a monkey wrench, and chased that spade crook for eight blocks, finally catching him, and telling him if he didn't return all the money and pay the cab fare as well, he was going to be wearing the wrench around his head for the rest of his life. P.S., the spade coughed up. I used to love his working nights. He'd get home for breakfast at eight in the morning, go to sleep, wake up at two, and then spend the rest of the day with me. I told all the kids he was a detective. He *looked* like a detective, you know? Well, his friends still call him Big Buono. Even now—hell, he's almost seventy—he can lift a refrigerator six inches off the floor. Strong as an ox. I love that guy. I just wish he'd get over this hang-up he has about his sister."

"What hang-up is that?" I asked.

"He thinks he killed her," Mary Margaret said.

"Oh."

"Actually, she died of scarlet fever, *every*body knows that, it's on the death certificate. But what happened was he'd gone for a walk with her the day before she took sick, and they got caught in a rainstorm, and then she came down with this fever of a hundred and four, and he figured it was because they got caught in the rain. Go tell him otherwise. He's yay big and yay wide, his friends call him Big Buono . . ."

"Yes, you told me that."

"But he still cries like a baby whenever he thinks back to that walk he and his kid sister took in the rain, and he tells anyone who'll listen that if it hadn't been for him, she'd still be alive today."

As Mary Margaret prattled on about the possible *real* reasons for her father's feelings of guilt (Had he, for example, seen his sister naked in the tub or copped a feel on the fire escape?) *I* considered the possibility that my *own* suppressed feelings of guilt were causing in me an unconscious clamoring for retribution, and that Rhoda (in the guise of Mary Margaret) satisfied this unfulfilled wish for punishment while simultaneously posing a threat that punishment might actually be meted, thereby causing extreme anxiety manifesting itself in the form of unreasoning fear—how do you like *that* one, Dr. Crackers? I rejected the possibility on the grounds that the resemblance to Rhoda had already been disproved, and besides, the whole guilt theory was Krakauer's, not mine. So why was I afraid of Mary Margaret? I asked silently, as I tilted yet another scotch on the rocks.

"I thought all that would change when he retired," Mary Margaret said. "I mean, a person can go crazy sitting in a cab all night with his own thoughts, don't you think? Especially when he keeps blaming himself for killing a nine-year-old kid. So when I started making such big money, I told him he could quit the cab, that I would take care of him, he could go to ball games, he could smoke his guinea stinkers, he could do whatever he liked from now on, without having to worry about a thing. The idea was to get him to stop thinking about his little sister all the time. So do you want to know what he does now? Instead of sitting in the *cab* and thinking about his sister, he sits in the *parlor* and thinks about her."

Mary Margaret shook her head. I, too, shook my head, but not in sympathy with her crazy old coot of a father. I shook it because I was still no closer to understanding why I considered her such a threat. She started to tell me about the eldest of her two brothers, something about him wanting to be a harness-race jockey (I *think* she said), another lunatic in a totally insane household—fifteen hundred bucks a week indeed! It suddenly occurred to me that Mary Margaret Buono was a call girl.

"Are you a call girl?" I asked.

"What?" she said, and burst out laughing. "Of course not," she said. "Who would pay me?"

"Then how do you earn fifteen hundred dollars a week?"

"Some weeks even more."

"How?"

"I'm a fashion model."

I now knew why I was afraid of Mary Margaret Buono. Mary Margaret Buono, as I had suspected all along, was completely and totally out of her bird.

"A fashion model," I said.

"Yes."

(What do you model? I wanted to ask. Circus tents?)

"I know what you're thinking," she said.

"Mm."

"You're thinking I'm not beautiful enough to be a fashion model."

"Why on earth would I think that?"

"Because it's true," Mary Margaret said. "But take a look at my hands."

I took a look at her hands. I am not an expert on hands, but I had certainly never seen lovelier hands in my life. From wrist to fingertip, from knuckle to joint, in length, width, girth, and depth, her hands were spectacularly beautiful. I fell immediately in love with her hands. I wanted to touch her hands and be touched by her hands, I wanted to sculpt her hands, I wanted to write sestinas about her hands, I wanted to go to bed with her hands. They did not seem to belong to her. You saw a pair of hands like that, and you expected someone tall and willowy and incredibly good-looking to be attached to them. You did not expect freckle-faced, pudgy, dumpy Mary Margaret to own those hands.

I once saw an old movie on television where a concert pianist had a terrible accident, and he lost his hands, and the surgeons gave him a pair of hands that used to belong to a strangler. So every time the pianist started to play Chopin, he got the urge to choke somebody. Looking at Mary Margaret's hands, I had the distinct impression that the operation had been performed on her in reverse. She was really a lady wrestler or a roller-derby champ, and she had lost her hands in a six-car collision, and they had grafted the hands of a dead harpist onto her wrists.

"Those are some hands," I said.

"They're my fortune. Anytime you see a pair of hands on a

television commercial or in a magazine ad, chances are they're mine."

"Those are really beautiful hands," I said.

"Yes, they are," she said, without false modesty. "I'm really impressed with them. I think I inherited them from my grandmother."

"Those are really the goddamnedest hands I've ever seen in my life."

"Yes, thank you."

"It's funny I didn't notice them before."

"Lots of people don't notice hands," Mary Margaret said.

"I've got very good-looking *feet*," I said. "But they're nothing compared to your hands."

"Well, thank you," she said.

"I'd be happy to show you my feet sometime, if you're interested."

"I'd love to see them right this minute," she said.

"In that case," I said, and reached down and unzipped first the right fur-lined boot and then the left fur-lined boot, and then took off first the right sock and then the left sock, and got off the bar stool, and put my feet close together and said, "*Voilà!*"

"They're extraordinary feet," Mary Margaret said.

"It's the arches," I said.

"And also the way the toes are angled. There's a very good gentle angle on the toes."

"Yes."

"I think I could develop a foot fetish for feet like those," she said.

"They are beautiful," I said.

"Does your grandmother have beautiful feet?"

"My grandmother is dead."

"I'm sorry."

"That's quite all right."

"Did she have beautiful feet when she was living?"

"I never had the pleasure of witnessing my grandmother's feet," I said.

"The only reason I ask . . ."

"Yes, is because . . ."

"Yes, because *my* grandmother had beautiful hands, you see . . ."

"Yes, I know."

"You've seen my grandmother's hands?"

"Never. I have never witnessed neither her hands nor my own grandmother's feet, may she rest in peace."

"Peter," she said, "I would like to propose a toast."

"Just let me get my socks back on," I said.

"What for? I love looking at your feet."

"Yes, but I don't want everyone in the place running over to kiss them. Now where'd I put . . . ? Okay. Okay."

"I would like to propose a toast to . . ."

"Just a minute, please."

"Did you see *The French Connection?*"

"Yes."

"Do you remember the scene where Popeye . . ."

"That's Faulkner."

"No, that's *The French Connection.*"

"The scene with the corncob?"

"No, the scene with the feet."

"Damn sock here doesn't seem to . . ."

"Where he arrests this man . . ."

"Must be the wrong damn foot."

"And asks him about his feet?"

"There we go."

"Anyway, here's a toast to . . ."

"Ooops, caught the little pinkie there."

"Do you want to hear this toast or not?"

"Just let me get this other one."

"What'd you say your grandmother's name was?"

"Grandma."

"Yes, mine too."

"There we are, all tucked away. What's the toast?"

"Here's to picking feet in Poughkeepsie."

"I don't get it," I said.

"I thought you saw *The French Connection.*"

"Yes, but dubbed in English."

"Oh," Mary Margaret said.

"You two are getting ossified," Robert said.

"You still owe me for my dress."

"What dress?"

"It cost me two dollars and fifty cents to have it dry cleaned."

"Huh?" Robert said.

"Robert," I said, "I think we need another round here."

"*I* think you need a week in the drunk tank."

"Robert's from California," Mary Margaret said.

"Two more of the same, please," I said.

"Which is where he learned how to ruin a girl's dress," Mary Margaret said.

"Huh?" Robert said, and went off for the drinks.

It occurred to me that I still didn't know why I was afraid of Mary Margaret. It also occurred to me that I *wasn't* afraid of her any more.

In my room, I curled up for a short nap and almost missed dinner. It was ten minutes to eight when I shook myself from total stupor and discovered that seven fire engines were racing to a false alarm inside my skull, bells clanging, sirens blowing and engines roaring. I staggered into the bathroom, took two Bufferin, went back to the bed, and collapsed on it. At eight twenty-five, I went into the bathroom again, this time to throw up. Outside the bathroom window, several wild animals were clawing at the pane and bellowing to be let inside. The fire engines in my head went wailing away into the distance, probably en route to Spanish Harlem. I hunched over the bowl in misery, remembering a time long ago when my father (in one of his more endearing moments) came home of a New Year's Eve and puked all over my bed. The smell of vomit had lingered in my nostrils till St. Swithin's Day, after which it rained for forty days and forty nights in accordance with tradition. I flushed the toilet.

The bedroom had somehow become affixed to the turntable of an extremely large record player. I stood in the exact center of the room, where the spindle poked up through the hole in the record, and I watched everything going by at thirty-three-and-a-third while I listened to a tune that sounded curiously like the Stones doing Shostakovich. The bed went by, the door went by, the dresser went by, the bathroom went by, the windows went by. It certainly was snowing out there. I decided I would have to find the Manual/Reject switch or else throw up again. (When your father thinks he's Ray Milland, you learn an awful lot about mice sticking their heads out of plaster cracks and being attacked by flying bats.) I had never before seen such an ugly bat with such gorgeous hands. Had I *really* exposed my feet to a passing subway train, thereby risking charges of indecent exposure, or had I only dreamt it? The windows went past again. It looked like one hell of a blizzard out there. The bed went past, and somebody knocked on it. "Who is it?" I asked, and watched the bathroom going by. "It's me," a voice said from the toilet bowl. "Who's me?" I asked the snowstorm, and the dresser answered, "David. Open up." I found the door on the third try, and discovered that by holding tightly to the knob I was able to go around *with* the

room instead of having *it* go around me. "What the hell's going
on in there?" David asked, and I said, "Just a minute, please,"
and debated whether I should let go of the knob with my
right hand in order to grab the bolt in order to unlock the
door, or whether I should continue hanging onto the knob and
try unlocking the door with my left hand, a feat of ambidexter-
ity that seemed light years beyond my capabilities of the moment. "Peter?" David said. "Yes, yes," I said, and made a stab
at the bolt with my left hand, missing, and decided to let go of
the knob. The room began to revolve again. I grabbed the
bolt with my right hand, seized the day as Chairman Mao and
President Nixon had earlier both advised, unlocked the door,
threw it open, and fell into David's arms.

"Oh, man," he said.

Considering my condition of not an hour before, it was
amazing that I could now sit in polite company around the
acorn fireplace in the intimate lounge and discuss the possibility that by tomorrow we might be snowbound. I had taken
a hot needlepoint shower at David's insistence and then had
dressed reluctantly for dinner, which I barely touched. Now
we sat talking (or rather *they* sat talking) about the fury of
the storm outside, *they* consisting of David, Sandy, and
Foderman. Foderman was upset. Foderman was a pain in the
ass, and he *always* was upset. He had still not heard from his
medical sidekick and erstwhile vaudeville partner, and was
afraid now that the storm might impair telephone service.
Sandy suggested that he could always send a carrier pigeon,
which Foderman did not find too terribly amusing. There is
only so much you can say about snowstorms and delinquent
telephone calls. I was about to suggest that if Foderman was
really so concerned about Schwartz, he should pick up a phone
and simply call his old buddy, but just then Mary Margaret

wandered into the lounge and over to our exciting little conversational group. I introduced her to the others, and then sat back with my arms folded across my chest, listening and watching, grateful (in my present state) for the opportunity to serve as spectator and recorder, rather than participant.

"Buono," Sandy said. "Is that Italian?"

"My father's Italian," Mary Margaret said. "My mother's Irish. That's where I get the red hair and the freckles."

"I thought the word was '*buoni*,'" David said. "*Ronzoni sono buoni.*"

"That's the plural."

"What does it mean?"

"Good."

"And *are* you good?" Sandy asked.

"When I'm good," Mary Margaret said, "I'm very very good," and smiled at Sandy. Sandy did not smile back. Mary Margaret looked suddenly bewildered.

"I once knew a neurosurgeon named Cativo," Foderman said. "Dr. Benjamin Cativo. That means 'bad' in Italian."

"No, that means 'evil,'" Mary Margaret said.

"Same difference," Foderman said, and shrugged.

"*I* once knew a doctor named Frankenstein," David said.

"Irving Frankenstein?" Sandy asked.

"Michael Frankenstein."

"On Seventy-ninth and Park?"

"No, in Transylvania."

"Pittsburgh, Transylvania?"

"That was Dracula, wasn't it?" Mary Margaret asked.

"Oh, was it?" Sandy said. "Really?"

"*What* was Dracula?" Foderman asked.

"A vampire," David said.

"You lost me," Foderman said, and shrugged again.

"We were discussing mad doctors as opposed to vampires," Sandy said.

"I sometimes think *all* doctors are mad," Foderman said, and chuckled. "Me included."

"Are you a doctor?" Mary Margaret asked.

"He's a gynecologist," Sandy said.

"If you're ever in the neighborhood, look him up," David said.

"Or vice versa," Sandy said, and Foderman burst out laughing.

"Why do people always make gynecologist jokes?" he asked. "Has anyone ever heard a *pediatrician* joke, for example?"

"I've never heard a gynecologist joke, either," Mary Margaret said.

"There are millions of them."

"Tell one," Mary Margaret said. "Please."

"Spare us," David said.

"Can *you* tell one, David?"

"I couldn't tell one from a hole in the ground."

"They all look the same to me, too," Sandy said.

"They got a lot of rhythm, though," David said.

"Especially in labor."

"You're laboring it, sweetie."

"Hasn't that been your experience?" Sandy asked.

"Hasn't *what* been my experience?" Foderman said.

"Contractions," Sandy said.

"It's," David answered. "Don't. Aren't. Isn't."

"Seriously," Mary Margaret said. "Do *any* of you know a gynecologist joke?"

"Nope," Sandy said, "but if you hum a few bars, I'll fake it."

"I've been to a few bars in my lifetime," David said, "and I hated them all."

"Bar none?"

"Bar One. Can't miss it. Big ranch over near the mesa."

"Mesa, mesa, come quick," Sandy said, "they's soldiers ober by de slabe quarters."

"I *still* don't know what you're talking about," Foderman said.

But Mary Margaret knew. Mary Margaret suddenly caught the pattern. The intelligence sparked in her level gaze, flashed out of her eyes as fiercely hot as the beam of the Green Lantern's ring. She leaned forward expectantly. She knew, and now she was ready to pounce, awaiting only the right opportunity. Sandy sensed her sudden knowledge, and her own electric-blue, twin-orbed radiation met Mary Margaret's virid beam of light; the challenge had been hurled, and now it would be met. With something close to interest, I observed.

"It doesn't look like we'll get any skiing in tomorrow," Foderman said, getting back to what he considered safe ground, a Ladies' Luncheon monologue entitled *Snowstorms I Have Known*. "I remember one time at Sugarbush, it snowed for three days and three nights. We couldn't budge from the hotel."

"I remember once in Italy," David said, "when it snowed in church in the middle of July."

"Really?" Sandy said. "When was that?"

"The fourteenth century. I don't remember it *personally*, of course, I was just a child at the time. But my mother recalled the incident to me. The whole family got caught in the snow, and I ruined my best rompers."

"It snowed right inside the church?" Sandy said.

"That's what happened."

"What church was that?"

"Santa Maria Cosa Nostra," David said.

"Did it snow hard?"

"Soft," David said. "Ordinary soft snow. Your regular garden variety snow."

"These two guys kill me," Foderman said. "I never know what they're talking about."

Mary Margaret waited and said nothing. From downstairs, in the larger lounge, we heard Max and his cronies beginning their nightly musical onslaught. Sandy, impatient to get this over with, anxious to know whether what had shown on Mary Margaret's face was truly recognition or merely something like anger or petulance, turned to her and said, "Do you speak Italian, Mary Margaret?"

"Nope," Mary Margaret said, and abruptly stood up. "Anybody feel like dancing?" she asked. "Seymour?"

"Why, yes, I think I'd like to," Foderman replied.

"See you," Mary Margaret said, and smiled briefly, and led Foderman out of the room.

I wasn't quite sure what had happened. We sat in silence, listening to the music from downstairs. Sandy was frowning. I had the feeling we'd been snubbed.

"Well, what do you want to do now?" David asked.

"Let's get out of here," Sandy said.

The Tiger Pit was one of the valley's discotheques, a sawdust saloon serving booze, beer, hamburgers and home fries. We came out of the howling snowstorm into the howling amplification of a four-piece rock group blasting at a mass of humanity packed elbows-to-buttocks. There was the smell of steamy garments, a huge open hearth blazing, a sign over the inner front door that read "No tiger in The Tiger Pit is hungrier than I"—a bastardization that undoubtedly caused old T. S. to revolve in his grave. The sound of the rock group was only slightly louder than the sound of the drinkers and dancers who, judging from the buttons on sweaters, parkas, and shirts, were all the Snowclad people in the world, assembled here to get Semanee and to get drunk besides. One crowd in particular stood out from the otherwise anonymous milling mass by virtue of its garb and its sheer decibel power. Lined up along the bar, singing and yelling a song that had nothing whatever to do with what the rock group was attempting to play, the men and women were dressed in male-female versions of the same basic uniform. The men were wearing green turtlenecks and ski pants, over which they had pulled on bright red swimming trunks. On the seat of each pair of trunks were the words "Merry Xmas" stitched in green. The women wore tight-fitting green leotards, right breast stitched in red with "Merry," left breast stitched with "Xmas." All, men and women alike, had bright Kelly-green plastic derbies on their heads. The song they were bellowing sounded like "God Rest Ye Merry Gentlemen." The "Get Semanee!" button was everywhere in evidence, pinned to trunks, belts, turtleneck collars, leotard tops, even—in the case of a delicious blond girl—one buttock of her ripe little ass.

My initial inclination was to get out of there fast. If there's one thing I can't stand, it's an "In" group, especially when I'm *out* of it. But Sandy spotted an empty table, immediately pushed through the crowd (David and I following, numbed by the sound), took off her parka as she bullied her way across the room, and grabbed the table an instant before a couple of starry-eyed teeny-boppers reached it. Tossing her parka onto one of the chairs, she sidled in behind the table with her back to the wall, smiled pleasantly at the two fifteen-year-olds, and then signaled for the waiter. David and I sat. The two little girls looked startled and indignant.

"Yes?" Sandy said.

"That was our table," one of the girls said.

"You're too young to drink," Sandy said flatly.

"We have I.D. cards," the other girl protested.

The waiter arrived at the table together with one of the Green Derbies, who had apparently spotted Sandy from the bar, and was wasting no time establishing a beachhead. He was a very large person. From where I was sitting, I estimated his height at six feet two inches and his weight at two hundred and forty. It was almost as though a sequoia had grown suddenly out of the sawdust. I have always wanted to be able to face another man and have him realize in an instant that he had better not start up with me unless he is feeling suicidal. The Green Derby standing by the table communicated this message at once. His sheer bulk was menacing, even though he was quite pleasant-looking, with a square, clean-shaven face and blond ringlets spilling from under the plastic derby, which he now removed from his head and held at his waist as he bowed formally and politely to the table. The teeny-boppers were still standing by, deciding whether or not to wet their pants. The waiter held pad and pencil at the ready. We were all anticipating the big fellow's speech. I was half-hoping a high-pitched squeak would come from his mouth. Grinning, slightly drunk, entirely ludicrous in his muscle-bulging turtle-neck, red swimming trunks and green ski pants, he said in a Western drawl, "My name's Bryan. Wanna dance?"

"Not right now, thanks," Sandy said. "I'd like a beer," she said to the waiter.

"They took our table," one of the little girls said, pleading to Bryan as a higher authority, probably because he was the biggest grown-up around.

"Too bad," Bryan said. "Whyn't you go home and watch *Sesame Street?*" He pulled out the fourth chair, and sat opposite David. I was sitting across from Sandy, and the two little girls were still standing at my elbow.

"They took our table," one of them said to the waiter.

"I've got one beer," the waiter said impatiently.

"Make it three," I said.

"Make it four," Bryan said.

"I'm going to tell the manager," the girl said.

"Go tell him," Sandy replied.

"Okay if I join you?" Bryan asked.

"You already have," Sandy said, and smiled.

"Big shots," the girl said, and she and her friend flounced away from the table.

"I didn't get your name," Bryan said.

"Sandy."

"Nice to meet you, Sandy. You're a beautiful girl."

"I'm Peter," I said.

"I'm David," David said.

Bryan greeted this unsolicited and volunteered information without much cheering or clapping. He leaned over the table, turned his back to me and his profile to David and addressed his next question (as he had his last) directly to Sandy, excluding both of us as effectively as if he'd built a wall of solid muscle.

"You staying here in the valley?" he asked her.

"Yes."

"Where?"

"At the Lodge," David said.

Bryan glanced at him briefly, and then turned back to Sandy. "Where?" he said again.

"At the Lodge," Sandy said.

"Must be an echo in this place," David said, and Bryan glanced at him again, and again turned away.

"Where are you from?" he asked Sandy.

"New York," I answered.

"New York," David said.

"And you?" Sandy asked.

"Arizona," Bryan said.

"Nice down there in Arizona," David said.

"You ever been there?" Bryan asked.

"Never. But I hear it's mighty nice down there."

"Yeah, it is," Bryan said.

"Mighty nice," I said.

Bryan stared first at me and then at David. There was a pained, perplexed and uncomprehending look on his face. Not the faintest spark of intelligence flared in his humorless eyes; he was as stupid as an oyster. Immediately (because I've always enjoyed trying to fathom the laborious thought processes of the intellectually underprivileged), I began amusing myself with fantasies of what he was possibly thinking (for lack of a better word). It seemed to me that Bryan felt he had stumbled upon a pair of Martians and was now ponderously debating whether he should squash us flat or attempt to learn our language. As he continued to stare at us, trying to understand the tight little smiles on our faces, the forbidding postures (backs rigid, arms folded across our chests), the seeming foolhardiness with which we were exercising our territorial imperative and protecting our turf from invasion, something vaguely resembling comprehension glimmered in his eyes. Expanding his private Martian reverie, Bryan was now doubtless weighing the possibility that our weaponry was far more sophisticated than his own. Was it not entirely possible that we were carrying death-ray guns that could reduce him to ashes on the spot? How else explain our reckless challenge to his superior strength? Were we crazy or something? Ah-*ha*, Bryan's eyes seemed to say. *That's* it. If they're not afraid of me, they've got to be nuts. And if they're nuts, I don't want nothing to do with them. (Duh, Bryan, very good, Bryan.)

Satisfied that he had tumbled to our secret, he promptly turned to Sandy again, one elbow on the table, grin widening as he prepared to launch into the second stanza of his seduction attempt, a tone poem that was interrupted by the untimely approach of the waiter. Sloshing foam and dripping perspiration, the waiter plunked four mugs of beer onto the tabletop and asked, "All on the same check?"

"Our friend here is paying," David said.

"Are you? Gee, thanks," Sandy said.

"Say, thanks a lot," I said.

"Huh?" Bryan said, and the waiter handed him the check.

"How much do you weigh?" I asked Bryan.

Bryan, frowning, staring at the check, said, "Two fifty-three."

"I guessed two forty."

"Give the man a kewpie doll," David said.

"Listen, whyn't you guys take a walk?" Bryan said.

"Snowing out there, Bryan," David said.

"Get our little bootsies wet," I said.

"I want to talk to the lady here," Bryan said.

"Go right ahead."

"Don't mind us."

"We'll just sit here and drink our little beersies," I said.

"Where'd you find these two guys?" Bryan asked Sandy.

"Are you a ski club or something?" David asked.

"What do you mean?"

"All the people in green derbies."

"The hats are just for fun," Bryan said. "We're down from Snowclad for the race tomorrow."

"Oh, are you racing?" I asked.

"No, but his motor's running pretty fast," David said, and Bryan shot him a warning look. I was, along about then, beginning to marvel at our audacity. Bryan was a very large person with a very small intelligence. Bryan was a dope, in fact, and I have always tried very hard to avoid contact with dopes. In my opinion, the dopes of the world are directly responsible and accountable for plague, pestilence, famine, warfare, racial strife, alienation, venereal disease, the high price of wheat, and the election of Richard M. Nixon. I have been known to cross deserts in the blistering sun rather than risk confrontation with a dope. So here we were in a sawdust saloon with a terrible rock group knocking down the walls, slurping beer and listening to a brainless jock pitching at Sandy while we sniped from the rooftops. What we were doing was dangerous. I began to realize just *how* dangerous it was, and felt a small tremor of excitement.

". . . minute you came in the door," Bryan was saying.

"Really? Why, thank you very much," Sandy said.

"Whyn't you finish your beer there, so we can dance?"

"Well, I like to sip beer slowly," Sandy said.

"What do you do for a living, Bryan?" David asked.

"I break horses."

"In half?" I said.

"Ever break a quarter horse in half?" David asked.

"You get an eighth of a horse that way," I said.

"What I do is I take wild horses and break them to the saddle," Bryan said.

"I wouldn't do that for all the money in the world," David said.

"Wild *horses* couldn't force me to do that," I said.

"It's fun," Bryan said, and once again dismissed us and turned to Sandy. "I'll bet you're a secretary or something back East," he said.

"How'd you guess?" Sandy asked.

"Just knew it right off."

"She works for the U.N.," David said.

"No kidding?"

"That's right," I said. "She's the Secretary General."

"Generally in charge of the secretarial pool," David said.

"Not to mention the beach," I said.

"We're trying to have a conversation here," Bryan said, and glared at us. But the chatter was beginning to reach him; he knew we were putting him on but he didn't know exactly how, and there was a vague uneasiness in his eyes. For a moment, I began to believe that the mild-mannered mathematicians of the world *could* actually triumph over the brutes and beasts without resorting to bear traps and boiling oil—but the odds changed quite suddenly. Bryan's two friends were somewhat bigger than he was. Wearing the same green derbies and red swimming trunks over green ski pants and green turtlenecks, they materialized at the table and one of them said, "Howdy, Bryan, who's your friend?"

"Hello, Duke. This here's Sandy."

"Nice to meet you, Sandy," Duke said. He had straight blond hair and light blue eyes. His nose had been broken more than once, either in barroom brawls or rodeos.

The fellow with him, dark-haired with small brown pig eyes and razor nicks on his throat and chin, reached across the table, took Sandy's hand, and said, "Let's dance, Sandy."

Sandy yanked her hand back. "I'm busy," she said.

"What with?"

"With *me*, Hollis," Bryan said.

"That right?" Hollis asked.

"No, that's wrong," Sandy said. "I'm busy with my friends."

"These little fellers your friends?" Hollis asked. The pair of them, Duke and Hollis, were standing at the corner of the table between Bryan and me, and casting very large shadows indeed. Hollis grinned down at me, and said, "Any friends of Sandy's is friends of mine," and extended a thick, beefy hand. "I'm Hollis," he said. "This here's Duke."

"I'm Peter," I said. "That there's David," and took the extended hand, fully expecting to retrieve it all mangled and

bent. But men who are confident of their power rarely display
it in meaningless shows of strength. Hollis shook my hand like
a proper gentleman, and then reached across the table and
offered David the same open palm.

"Hello, David," he said, "I'm Hollis."

"Nice to meet you, Hollis."

"My pleasure," Hollis said. "This here's Duke."

"Howdy, David and Peter."

"Howdy, Duke," I said.

"Getting mighty crowded around here," Bryan said.

"Now, that ain't sociable, Bryan," Hollis said. "Besides, these
two gentlemen here was just now preparing to leave. Ain't that
right, boys?"

"No," David said, "that *ain't* right, Hollis."

"Funny," Hollis said, "I thought I heard you say you was
going for a walk or something."

"Bryan," I said, "why don't you and your friends go back to
the bar and give us a chorus of 'Silent Night.'"

"The silenter the better," David said.

"Good night, boys," Sandy said.

"See you around the pool hall," I said.

"You *got* to be kidding," Hollis said.

Yes, I thought, we are kidding. We certainly have no intention of starting up with you stupid cowboys. Holy Trinity
aside, we recognize the full potential of your physical advan-
tage, and are decidedly eager to avoid broken heads and
bloody noses, not to mention whatever it is you have in mind
for Sandy. We are kidding, gentlemen. We have pushed this
little charade a bit too far, and will probably have ample opportunity to regret our rashness during a long and painful
hospital recovery. We are all kidding here (heh-heh), can't
you take a little joke, fellers? Whyn't you all wander on back
to the corral and break a few horses, huh?

"We're not kidding," I said. "Now shove off."

The only time I ever received a beating in my life was when I was fourteen years old and called my father an irresponsible (or perhaps irrepressible) drunk. He took off his belt and beat me so hard I couldn't walk for three days. He also blackened both my eyes with his fists. (Need I mention that he was drunk at the time?) Beatings are not much fun. Fantasies of being tossed around by Bryan and Company (perhaps even being buggered by them after they had broken all our bones) flashed through my head like the last images of a drowning man. I guess I expected Sandy to save the day. I don't know why. I guess I expected her to say something or do something that would send these three hulking horse wrestlers back to the bar. But Sandy remained silent, and one look at her face (blue eyes wide, lips trembling) told me she was just as frightened as I. So who was going to save us? David? I looked at David. David was not going to save us.

Oddly, I began wishing Dr. Krakauer were there. Patiently but firmly, Dr. Krakauer would tell these three dopes that violence solves nothing. David and I, he would say to the cowboys, were just two fun-loving kids from Manhattan, out here to have ourselves a good time, certainly intending no harm to our western neighbors, farthest thing from our minds. Feelings of hostility, the good doctor would explain, were sometimes inexplicably present in chance encounters between strangers, but outward expression of such urges was contra-indicated and highly inappropriate. (That will be a hundred and twenty dollars, please. Forty dollars for each of you.)

The silence lengthened.

Dr. Krakauer did not appear on a winged couch.

Instead, from the door, there came an instantly recognizable voice, proving to my satisfaction that God is a woman.

"Hey there, Bryan!" Mary Margaret shouted. "How you doing, cowboy?"

Green parka wet with snow, face raw from the wind outside, red hair tangled and limp, she came toward the table with Foderman not a foot behind her, arms wide in offered embrace as Bryan, grinning, got immediately to his feet.

"Well, I'll be shat upon!" he said, and lifted Mary Margaret off her feet in a fierce bear hug. "You're back!"

"I'm back," she said. "Put me down, you big ox!"

"You should be up at Snowclad," he said. "Deader'n a doornail down here."

"Not any more, it isn't," Mary Margaret said. "Hey, hi, Peter!"

"You know these guys?" Bryan asked, and blinked.

"Oh, sure, good friends of mine," Mary Margaret said. "Hi, David, hi, Sandy. Who're *these* two hulking monsters?" she asked, and poked her forefinger at Hollis's bulging left pectoral. Hollis flinched, protectively covering his chest with both hands, like a virgin who'd just been molested on the subway.

Laughing, Bryan said, "That's Duke and Hollis. *Damn*, it's good to see you!"

"Let's get a bigger table," Mary Margaret said. "This is Seymour Foderman, from the Bronx."

"Hello," Foderman said, and smiled.

Our little party started in the back room of The Tiger Pit, at the bigger table Mary Margaret demanded. That was around eleven-thirty, when there were still seven of us. By a quarter to one, there were nine of us. It was a very peculiar party. It left us shaken and depressed, which is probably why Sandy, David, and I went to bed together afterwards.

Dr. Krakauer once hinted darkly that David and I in bed together with Sandy constitutes a symbolic homosexual act.

Everything is homosexual to Dr. Krakauer. Shake hands with your minister, that's homosexual. Pass the salt, that's homosexual. I suggested to Dr. Krakauer that perhaps he had not personally resolved his own feelings of masculine inadequacy, and, true to form, he replied, "Perhaps not." When I reported to Sandy that Krakauer thought she was a beard for a pair of fags, she unzipped my fly and blew me. (I did not report this incident to the herr doktor because he probably would have found *it* homosexual as well.) Good old Crackers. He should have been at the party. He'd have instantly committed both Foderman and Mary Margaret, who began revealing aspects of their personalities that had until then been almost totally hidden.

Foderman, I decided, was a masochist.

Mary Margaret, I decided, was a monster.

Alone together on a desert island, they might have effected a splendid marriage, Mary Margaret slowly whittling away, Foderman shrieking in ecstasy each time she approached him with a carving knife. But the presence of the Green Derbies (and later the two teeny-boppers) proved catalytic, providing for Foderman and Mary Margaret just the proper indulgent environment they both craved. Mary Margaret now had the audience of noted scientists necessary for the proper appreciation of her experiment. Foderman, strapped to the table without benefit of anesthesia, lifted his head and peered through the glare of the overhead lights, dimly aware of that same audience, and secretly pleased to be the prime object of their attention. Even later, when he lay there on the reddening sheet, sliced open from Adam's apple to scrotum, he misunderstood the cheering and thought the applause was for his exposed guts rather than for the brilliant, mad surgeon who had performed the operation. As I said, it was a very peculiar party.

By way of openers (scalpel, please), Mary Margaret asked Bryan if they had any Jews down there in Arizona where he came from, and Bryan answered Why, sure, there's Jews down there, why Barry Goldwater's a Jew, ain't he? Foderman nodded and said there were Jews all over the United States, and then smiled and said, "Though, probably, in lots of little southern and western towns, the people think we've got horns and a tail."

"Nobody thinks that in Arizona," Bryan said.

"Well," Foderman said, and shrugged.

"Listen, how'd we get talking about Jews?" Mary Margaret said, and patted Foderman's hand comfortingly, and then said, "Why don't we order some drinks?"

A series of cross-conversations developed at the table, Bryan and Mary Margaret reminiscing about the good times they'd had here together last year, Hollis and Duke telling Sandy about the joys of living in the open and eating baked beans cooked over a small fire, and Foderman telling David and me that he had finally heard from the good doctor Schwartz, the call coming scant moments before he and Mary Margaret left the hotel. The result was a Robert Altman movie.

KR: I'm interested in this concept of yourself as the star of a movie.

ME: I never said that.

KR: You've repeatedly told me you have difficulty reconciling reality with fantasy.

ME: I said I sometimes feel out of it.

KR: Out of what?

ME: What's happening.

KR: What do you suppose is happening?

ME: I don't follow you.

KR: What do you suppose you're missing?

ME: I still don't follow you.

KR: If I understand you correctly, you think something's going on behind your back.

ME: No.

KR: Then, what?

ME: What I said was that sometimes I walk along the street at night and see lighted windows in apartment buildings, and wonder what's happening in those apartments.

KR: What do you *suppose* is happening in those apartments?

ME: How would I know? People are living in them, I suppose.

KR: And doing what?

ME: What do you want me to say? That they're in there fucking?

KR: Are they?

ME: I suppose so, yes. And they're also eating and reading and brushing their teeth and watching television and whatever the hell else people do in their own houses.

KR: But primarily fucking.

ME: No, *not* primarily fucking.

KR: Then, what?

ME: Talking.

KR: About what?

ME: I don't know what.

KR: Try to imagine their conversation.

ME: No. I don't know what other people talk about.

KR: What do you and Sandy and David talk about?

ME: Everything.

KR: I don't mean when you're talking code.

ME: Code? What code?

KR: The code you use when you're together.

ME: We don't have any code.

KR: I think it's a code. The same kind of code little children use in imitation of a foreign language. Have you ever used such a code?

ME: No.

KR: Pig Latin? Or adding vowels or consonants to disguise true meaning? Like Pa-Peter Pa-Piper pa-picked a pa-peck of pa-pickled pa-peppers.

ME: That's a great code. How'd you ever crack it?

KR: The children using it think it's indecipherable to outsiders.

ME: Well, we don't have any code like that. We talk straight English to each other.

KR: It's more like a shorthand English, isn't it?

ME: Yes, right. We know each other so well, we can cut corners. We don't have to spell everything out.

KR: I don't think you know each other at all.

ME: What's that supposed to mean?

KR: I think you deliberately use this code of yours . . .

ME: I told you we don't have . . .

KR: Very well, this shorthand English of yours . . .

ME: Right.

KR: I think you use it to *avoid* communication.

ME: Why would we do that?

KR: When's the last time you had a *real* conversation with anyone?

ME: Yesterday.

KR: With whom?

ME: Sandy. On the telephone.

KR: She called from Bennington?

ME: I called *her*.

KR: What did you talk about?

ME: I wanted to know when she was coming down.

KR: You already *know* when she's coming down. She's

coming down on December twelfth. Six days from
now.

ME: I wanted to make sure.

KR: Do you always check her movements so closely?

ME: No, but we're supposed to be leaving for Semanee on
the sixteenth, and I just wanted to make sure everything was all set.

KR: Do you have trepidations about the trip?

ME: None. I'm looking forward to it.

KR: You'll be missing more than two weeks here.

ME: I'll survive.

KR: Will you?

ME: Come on, Doctor, cut it out. I'm not *dependent* on
these goddamn sessions. I can function quite well
without them.

KR: Good.

ME: You don't believe me, do you?

KR: I do believe you. In fact, I'm pleased you think we're
making progress.

ME: I didn't say that.

KR: *Don't* you think we're making progress?

ME: You're the doctor, Doctor.

KR: I think we're making progress.

ME: That's the nicest thing you've said to me all week.

KR: Then, why do you respond to it with sarcasm?

ME: That wasn't sarcasm.

KR: Perhaps not. Perhaps you're only using code again.

". . . going to be all right," Foderman said. "In fact, he's
been invited to a party on New Year's Eve."

"Who's that?" Mary Margaret asked, turning suddenly from
Bryan.

"Schwartz," Foderman replied. "My friend. The one who
called me just before we came over here."

"I admire the way Jews stick together," Mary Margaret said conversationally.

"Well, it's a necessity sometimes," Foderman said.

"You never camped out, huh?" Hollis asked Sandy.

"Never," Sandy said.

"Didn't belong to the Girl Scouts or nothing?"

"*Hated* the Girl Scouts."

"Because of persecution, do you mean?" Mary Margaret asked.

"Yes, certainly," Foderman said. "When you're forced to live in a ghetto . . ."

"What's a ghetto?" Bryan asked.

"Knock, knock," I said to David.

"Who's there?"

"Ghetto."

"Ghetto who?"

"Ghetto you ass inna here, Luigi."

"I no ghetto the joke," David said.

"What the hell's a ghetto?" Bryan asked.

"You're in your sleeping bag with them stars up there," Hollis said, "and, man, you feel like a million bucks. You don't need nothing else in the world. Just that fire to keep the wildcats off your back, and that nice warm bag, and them stars winking down. Ain't nothing like it in the whole world."

"Remember that night last year when we sacked out on the mountain?" Bryan asked. "And skied down just as the sun was coming up? Like to froze our asses off."

"That was fun, that night," Mary Margaret said. "Are you a good skier, Seymour?"

"I'm an Advanced Intermediate," Foderman said. "Well, ask *them.*"

"Is he?" Mary Margaret said.

"He's coming along," David said.

"I had a bad day yesterday, I'll admit . . ."

"Because your bindings weren't adjusted properly," Sandy said.

"That must've been it," Foderman said.

"Maybe we can all ski together tomorrow," Mary Margaret said.

"We're heading back to Snowclad right after the race," Bryan said.

"If this snow keeps up," Foderman said, *"nobody'll* be skiing tomorrow."

"What time's the race?" I asked.

"Ten in the morning," Hollis said.

"Well, then, maybe just the five of us," Mary Margaret said. "That okay with you, Seymour?"

"Oh, sure," Foderman said. "If you can keep up with these three. They're very good skiers."

"Have you been over to the north face?"

"Not yet."

"I'd love to take you there," Mary Margaret said.

"We skied the north face a lot last year," Bryan said.

"That's mighty hairy territory over there," Hollis said.

"You can disappear from sight there, and never be heard from since," Duke said.

"What do you mean?" Foderman asked.

"That's the only place I ever skied where I had the feeling I could fall *off* the mountain. You understand me? Not *down* the mountain, but *off* it."

"Is it *that* steep?"

"It's steep, all right."

"The trails run clear around these deep canyons. You miss a turn, and that's *it*, pal."

"Aren't there guard rails or something?" Foderman asked.

"*Guard* rails?" Duke asked incredulously, and burst out laughing.

"Now don't get frightened, Seymour," Mary Margaret said.

"I'm not frightened, I'm just curious."

"There are places on the north face," Hollis said, "where I swear to God the trail's only as wide as your own two skis. You feel like a goddamn mountain goat hanging on with your toe-nails."

"They're trying to scare you, Seymour," Mary Margaret said.

"No, no, listen, who's scared?"

"You go over the edge of one of them sheer drops, and it's not like a skier taking a fall, it's like a mountain climber whose rope just snapped. You sail out into space, and you grab for sky, and if you're lucky you get stopped by a tree or a boulder a mile below. By that time, it don't matter no more because you're busted in a million pieces anyway."

"Sure you want to go over there, Seymour?" Mary Margaret asked.

"Why not?" Foderman asked. "I'm not scared."

"*I'm* scared," David said.

"Me, too," I said.

"I got to tell you," Bryan said, "I've skied most places in the world . . ."

"Oh, sure," Mary Margaret said.

"You think I'm kidding you? I've skied Europe, I've skied Australia, I've even skied Chile. But last year on that north face, I had a lot of trouble keeping a tight asshole."

"They're telling you atrocity stories, Seymour," Mary Margaret said.

"You think I don't know it? It's the old Army hypodermic routine. The needle with a propeller on the end."

"You're gonna *wish* you had a propeller on your end," Duke said.

"And *wings*," Hollis said.

"Well, I'll give it a try anyway," Foderman said. "Even without a propeller. What can I lose?"

"Your life," Bryan said.

"Come on, come on," Foderman said. "My life."

"Seymour's people are used to all sorts of danger and hardship," Mary Margaret said.

"This ain't the same as being taken to the ovens," Duke said. "Here you got a choice whether to go or not."

"They had a choice there, too, didn't they?" Mary Margaret asked.

"What choice?" Foderman said.

"They could have refused."

"How? How can you refuse to get in a boxcar when somebody's holding a machine gun on you?"

"It's a matter of how you choose to die."

"No, it's a matter of hope. If you get on the train, then maybe something will happen on the way. Maybe the war will end, maybe the train will crash, you'll escape . . ."

"Bullshit," Mary Margaret said.

"What would *you* have done?" Sandy asked flatly.

"I'd have refused to go," Mary Margaret said.

"And they'd have shot you," Foderman said.

"All right. At least, I'd have taken a stand."

"For what? If they shot you, you were dead. You think it mattered to them, another dead Jew? Jews weren't people to them. Listen, don't get me started. This is a subject I can't discuss unemotionally. All this business of what you would have done, what you wouldn't have done. This was *survival,* they did what they could to *survive.* None of us here knows a thing about survival, so what are we talking about?"

"*I* know about survival," Bryan said.

"All right, so you know about it. Let's change the subject."

"In the Army, I learned all about survival."

"So did I," Hollis said.

"Were you in the Army, Seymour?" Mary Margaret asked.

"Yes, I was in the Army."

"See any action?"

"I was attached to a field hospital."

"Ever kill anybody?" Duke asked.

"No. My job was saving people, not killing them."

"Was your life ever in danger?"

"Never."

"Then what do you know about survival?"

"I was dealing with survival every day of the week. A man comes into the hospital with his legs blown off and his intestines hanging out . . ."

"*Please,*" Mary Margaret said.

"I'm sorry, but that was an everyday fact of life. *That* was survival."

"But not *your* survival."

"The survival of another human being *is* my survival."

"Seymour's a doctor," Mary Margaret said.

"I gathered," Bryan said. "You a G.P.?"

"I'm a gynecologist," Foderman said, and Bryan burst out laughing. "What's so funny about that?"

"Just seems like a big change," Bryan said. "From handling a man's intestines to handling a lady's privates."

"I prefer it," Foderman said with dignity.

"Who wouldn't?" Duke said.

"Anyway," Mary Margaret said, "do we try the north face or not?"

"Of course, we try it," Foderman said. His face was flushed, and his pale eyes looked feverish. I had the strangest feeling he was about to cry.

"I'm not sure Seymour's a good enough skier," I said.

"He just told us he's an Advanced Intermediate," Mary Margaret said.

"I am," Foderman said.

"Those sound like expert trails to me."

"And Seymour's no expert," David said.

"I can manage, don't worry," Foderman said.

"They *are* expert trails, aren't they?" I asked Bryan.

"Yeah, but he can probably handle them. All it takes is a little guts, that's all."

"How are you in the guts department?" Mary Margaret asked.

"I'm not afraid of the mountain," Foderman said.

"What *are* you afraid of?"

"A great many things. But not the mountain."

"What?"

"Pain? Suffering?" Foderman shrugged.

"You fall off that north face," Hollis said, "you're gonna know pain *and* suffering both."

"I don't intend to fall off," Foderman said.

"Now, there's a brave man for you," Mary Margaret said. She raised her glass and said, "I drink to this brave man here."

"Ain't no such thing as a brave man," Bryan said. "I learned that in the Army, too. All there is is cowards who learn how to live with their own fear."

"I think you're right," Foderman said.

"Oh, are you a coward, Seymour?" Mary Margaret asked.

"In many ways, yes."

"In that case, I drink to this coward here," Mary Margaret said. "Here's hoping nobody ever holds a machine gun on you and asks you to get into a boxcar."

I did not honestly know how Mary Margaret had led the conversation back full circle again to the annihilation of Jews in Germany, especially after Foderman had expressed his aversion to the subject. I knew only that she was somehow equating gas chambers with mountains, intimating that if Foderman refused the challenge of the north face, his decision would be tantamount to stepping voluntarily (and cowardly) into an oven. But Foderman had already stated that he was *not* afraid of the mountain and that indeed he was ready and willing to try it tomorrow. So what the hell was she driving at? It further seemed to me that if Foderman skied the north face, he was placing himself in an extraordinarily dangerous position. I did not want to hurt his feelings (he seemed besieged enough already), but I felt it was necessary to try to dissuade him.

"Seymour," I said, "I think you'd better reconsider."

"Yeah, Seymour," David said.

"Reconsider what?"

"The north face."

"That's already settled," Foderman said.

"Seymour," I said flatly, "you don't ski well enough."

"I'm an Advanced Intermediate," Foderman said.

"You're a notch above a Beginner," I said. "And those are expert trails over there."

"If you don't mind, Peter," Foderman said, "I'll make my own decision, thank you."

"Bravo," Mary Margaret said.

"Mary Margaret," I said, "I think you ought to keep out of this. He can hurt himself badly over there."

"He can hurt himself crossing the street, too."

"That's not the same thing, and you know it."

"I got to tell you," Bryan said, "this is beginning to bore the ass off of me. I don't care whether Seymour skis the north face or the Matterhorn. I'm interested in doing a little serious drinking and having a little fun. Now, whyn't you just let him make up his own damn mind?"

"Right," Mary Margaret said. "If he's afraid of the . . ."

"I'm *not* afraid," Foderman said.

"Then what are we arguing about?"

"I have no idea," Foderman said. "The matter is settled."

"Sandy?" I said.

Sandy, who had been mostly silent until now, looked first at Foderman, and then at Mary Margaret. Shrugging, she said, "It's his funeral."

"Exactly," Mary Margaret said, and smiled.

It had stopped snowing by a quarter to one, when we came out of The Tiger Pit and headed up the street for Maury's West, a joint allegedly owned and operated by a former Yale man who'd apparently lost his way. The wind had almost died, and the sky was streaked with scudding clouds, the tattered remnants of the storm. Hollis looked up, took a deep breath, and said, "This's what it's like out there in the open, Sandy. All them zillions of stars dripping their shine on you. It's just about more'n a man can . . ."

A snowball smashed into the back of his head before he could finish the sentence, knocking his Stetson into the street. He whirled with fists clenched, saw no one, said, "Now, what the hell?", put his hands on his hips, and then heard muffled laughter behind one of the snowbanks. He went directly up over the top of the bank, digging in the toes of his boots, disappeared for a moment, and then came back into the street dragging two giggling girls whom I recognized instantly as the teeny-boppers whose table we'd usurped. "Look what I got here, Bryan," he said, and Bryan turned from Mary Margaret and said, "Throw 'em back in the pond, Hollis. They're too little."

"We're eighteen," one of the girls said.

"Almost nineteen," the other one said.

"Like hell you are," Mary Margaret said.

"They look plenty big enough to me," Hollis said.

"Where you looking, cowboy?" the first girl said, and grinned.

"All over, honey," Hollis answered. "What's your name?"

"Taffy," she said.

"Mmm-*mmm*," Hollis said. "And yours?"

"Annabelle."

"Well, well," Hollis said.

"That's jail bait, Hollis," Duke advised.

"Girls said they were eighteen, didn't they?"

"They're scarcely out of puberty," Foderman remarked drily.

"Let 'em go, Hollis," Bryan said. "Their mothers'll be out looking for them."

"We're here alone," Annabelle said.

"Our mothers are in San Francisco," Taffy said.

"Well, well," Hollis said.

"And we've got I.D. cards," Annabelle said.

"Whose?" Mary Margaret asked.

"What difference does it make? We've got 'em, that's all that counts."

"I'm going back to the hotel," Foderman said. "I'll see you fellows in San Quentin."

"Hey, come *on*, Seymour," Mary Margaret said. "You're my date."

"I thought *I* was your date," Bryan said.

"First come, first served."

"I voluntarily relinquish all claims," Foderman said. "Besides, if we're going to ski the north face tomorrow . . ."

"Seymour, I absolutely refuse to let you go," Mary Margaret said.

"Where're we going?" Taffy asked.

"Just up the street here, honey."

"To play jacks," Foderman said, which was the second such zinger he'd hurled in the past few minutes. I was beginning to think it was possible he possessed a sense of humor.

"Seymour," Mary Margaret said warningly, and walked directly up to him, and put her face close to his, and said, "if you leave me alone with this big ape here . . ."

"Listen to the ungrateful bitch," Bryan said, and laughed.

"I'll never forgive you as long as I live."

"Taught her everything she knows," Bryan said, still laughing.

"Is anybody holding?" Annabelle asked.

"Holding *what?*" Duke said.

"Grass," Annabelle said.

"Oh, Jesus," Sandy said, and shook her head. "If nobody minds, I think *I'll* go to sleep, too. Come on, Seymour."

"Grass?" Duke said. "Did she say grass?"

"Grass, Duke," Mary Margaret said. "What the cows eat."

"Grass?"

"Forget it, Duke."

"Well, *is* anybody holding?" Annabelle asked.

Taffy, apparently bored with the conversation, decided to lift the proceedings to a higher level by making another snowball and hurling it directly at Hollis's head. Hollis ducked the throw, and then scampered after her up the side of a twelve-foot-high snowbank left by the plows. Taffy whirled, put both hands on Hollis's chest, and gave him a push that sent him sliding back down the side of the bank.

"King of the mountain!" she shouted. "Try to get me off!"

"Who're your friends, Peter?" Sandy whispered.

"I thought they were with you," I whispered back.

"When do we start finger painting?" David asked.

Bryan was running up the side of the bank, eager to answer this challenge to his manhood. No mere little slip of a thing was going to stand on top of that hill while Bryan the Breaker was there to knock her off. Bellowing the way he probably did at recalcitrant ponies, he seized her wrist, swung her around, and sent her flying head over teacups to the bottom. Taffy shrieked in ecstasy and fear. Annabelle, who'd apparently forgotten how sophisticated it was to ask if anyone was in possession of marijuana, danced a little excited jig in the snow. Bryan pounded his chest like King Kong on top of the Empire State, and bellowed, "Come on, you chicken flickers!", and Hollis and Duke, responding predictably, raced up the hill to engage him in combat. There ensued one of those brief homosexual (god*damn* that Dr. Crackers!) displays of masculine grunting, groaning, and grappling usually confined to the locker room and accompanied by buttocks-flicking whips of a wet towel, but here enacted on a high hill in the open air, thereby dignifying it as a contest of physical endurance. Boys will be boys. Bryan grabbed Hollis by the seat of his swimming trunks and the collar of his parka and tossed him down the hill summarily, Hollis laughing all the way to the bottom. Duke wrestled briefly with Bryan, caught him in a headlock, yanked him off his feet, twisted him around, and sent him tripping backwards, arms flailing, toward the plowed street, where the rest of us greeted his arrival without ceremony.

"Go get him, Seymour!" Mary Margaret said.

"Don't be ridiculous," Foderman answered.

"King of the mountain, king of the mountain!" Duke shouted.

"You afraid of him?" Mary Margaret said.

"No."

"Then, go knock him off that hill!"

"Why?"

"Why not?" Mary Margaret said.

I thought Foderman would have at his fingertips at least a

thousand good reasons for not going up that hill. But instead of replying, possibly confusing the hill with a boxcar and remembering the earlier image of an S.S. man holding a machine gun on a herd of submissive Jews, he merely shrugged and started up toward where Duke, legs spread, arms hanging at his sides like a gunslick ready to draw, was waiting for him. Foderman's technique for going up a hill was the same one he used for coming down a hill. He merely moved on a straight line, like a tank heading for a distant objective. *Chomp, chomp, chomp,* he chewed the hill level, grabbed for Duke's ankles, pulled him over even as he himself rolled aside to avoid the falling timber, and then scrambled to his feet and claimed the summit before Duke rolled to a snow-spitting stop at the bottom. As Duke climbed to his feet again and stared up in disbelief at Foderman, Mary Margaret took Bryan aside and whispered something in his ear. Bryan nodded, grinned, and then went into an old-fashioned football huddle with his cowboy chums, arms intertwined, heads close together. At the top of the hill, Foderman waited apprehensively.

From three sides of the snowbank now, like the lead rifleman and twin grenadiers of an enemy patrol, Bryan, Duke, and Hollis started up in triangular formation, approaching Foderman, who stood looking down at them with a slightly bewildered expression on his face. He had taken the high ground without casualty and now found himself in the embarrassing position of having to defend a worthless piece of real estate against an army that had no more use for it than he had. It must have crossed his mind that this was a senseless battle in a war not of his choosing, and yet could he surrender without at least some show of resistance? Could he let them herd him into a boxcar and stuff him into an oven without protest? He clenched his fists in resolve. Short, stubby, breathless, barrel-shaped, he stood atop the ramparts of his mountain fortress, a pitiful, helpless slob awaiting the onslaught of a dedicated demolition team.

What happened next surprised me completely.

I had expected the three cowboys to toss Foderman into the air like a beanbag and then hurl him down to the street below. But instead, approaching from three sides to reach the summit simultaneously, they reached for his ankles, his legs, and his waist and, working silently and in concert, pulled his ski pants down to his boots, and swiftly retreated to the bottom of the hill. Foderman registered first surprise, and then what seemed to be relief, or even gratitude. They had *not* sent mortars into his castle keep, they had *not* used flamethrowers or grenades, he had *not* been routed, raped, or even ransacked. He was, in fact, still king of the mountain, however lacking in regality he may have appeared to the populace assembled below, his pants pulled down, his bare legs hanging out, and his undershorts blowing in the breeze. He didn't seem to know quite how to cope with the indignity of his disarray. Bewildered, and a little chilly besides, he waited for some guidance from the people, some cue from the street below.

It was Mary Margaret who began laughing.

The laughter bubbled up out of her throat like a tainted underground spring, clear and cold and sparkling, but deadly to the palate. The teeny-boppers came in not a beat behind, shrilling like treetop birds, and Bryan, Duke, and Hollis belatedly brayed accompaniment until the entire valley seemed to reverberate with laughter that rose to the crest of the hill, where it completely engulfed Foderman. He hesitated. He still did not pull up his pants. A smile broke on his face, and a timid laugh escaped his lips, followed by a louder laugh, and then another. Clasping his hands over his head like a prizefighter who had just won the world's championship, he nodded, laughed more heartily, and shook his wedded, scepterless mitts at all of us below. Bryan and Duke could barely remain standing. Each slapping the other's back, they stumbled about drunkenly in the snow, and Mary Margaret's chilling laughter broke on the air like falling icicles, and the teeny-boppers applauded, and Hollis threw his Stetson to the ground and jumped up and down on it, while Foderman stood with his hands over his head and his pants around his ankles, laughing.

I think the saddest sound I ever heard in my life was the sound of Foderman laughing that night.

We got back to the hotel shortly after one o'clock. Mary Margaret had elected to go on to Maury's with the cowboys and the kids, and Foderman had finally managed to pull up his pants before frostbite attacked his extremities. He now promised to meet us at nine for breakfast, and went directly to his room. Alice was curled up in one of the big leather lobby chairs, with Helmut the drummer sitting on the arm of it and telling her how crappy the skiing was in America. She barely glanced at me as I followed David and Sandy toward the small lounge, where the action consisted solely of Mr. and Mrs. Penn R. Trate sitting by the acorn fireplace, heads together in apparent connubial bliss. Wearily, we went upstairs to Sandy's room.

There was no question of us separating for the night, there was no need even to discuss it. All three of us were still confused and, yes, shocked, by what had just happened in the snow outside, and we felt the need to talk about it, sort it out and make some sense of it. Mary Margaret seemed a threat, and there was a need to reaffirm our contiguousness, a desperate urgency to touch again—touch minds, touch bodies, assure ourselves that we were still an inseparable, impervious, indivisible unit. Completely at ease in each other's presence, we talked quietly as we got ready for bed, David sitting in one of the chairs to take off his boots, Sandy unbuttoning her blouse, I going into the john to pee, leaving the door open so I could hear the conversation and share in it.

"That's the first anti-Semite I ever met in my life," David said. "I thought they'd gone out of style."

"Why'd he stand still for it?" Sandy asked.

"Because he's a shmuck," I said from the bathroom.

"She sure does take control of a situation, doesn't she?"

"Listen, it's a good thing she arrived when she did. I think we were about to get pulverized."

"I didn't know they grew them so big in Arizona," I said.

"You going to be in there all night, Peter?"

"How'd you like Bryan not knowing what a ghetto is?"

"Hurry *up*, Peter!"

"All right, all right."

I came back into the bedroom, and David, barefooted, went into the john. Sandy, wearing only her slacks, was studying one of her breasts in the mirror, her hand cupped under it.

"What's this?" she asked me.

"What?"

"This? Is it anything?"

"It looks like a little bruise."

"Mmm," she said. She looked worried.

"I don't think it's anything," I said, and went to the bed and took off my boots and socks. "Why do you suppose she went after him that way?"

"She's a Jew-baiter, that's why," Sandy said.

"You think that's all?"

From the bathroom, David said, "Okay to use your tooth-brush, Sandy?"

"What?"

"Your toothbrush."

"Yeah, sure. But what's she *after?* If she doesn't like Sey-mour, why does she want to ski with him?"

"She's a model, did you know that?"

"Who?"

"Mary Margaret."

"What does she model?"

"Jock straps," David said from the bathroom, and spit into the sink.

"Her hands," I said.

"Yeah?" Sandy said.

"She's got beautiful hands."

"I didn't notice."

"Peter, why don't you go get us some pajamas?"

"What do we need pajamas for?"

"Gets mighty cold out here on the tundra," David said, and spit into the sink again.

"Where's your key?"

"On the dresser there. Near my wallet."

"Are we really going to ski with them tomorrow?"

"Not with her," Sandy said.

"You suppose she's a good skier?" David asked, and came out of the bathroom.

"She's very good. I saw her one morning."

"You still here?"

"Why don't you go get your own pajamas?"

"I'm barefoot."

"So am I."

"Is this anything?" Sandy asked, and showed David the bruise.

"Go ask Dr. Foderman."

"Why didn't he pull up his pants?" I asked.

"Maybe he *likes* them half-mast," David said.

"Did you dig those shorts of his?"

"My father wears shorts like that," I said.

"I'm surprised he wasn't wearing garters."

"Garters cause varicose veins."

"Who told you that?"

"Scientific fact," David said, and took off his pants. "Anybody mind if I open the window a little?"

"I thought you were worried about the tundra."

"It's unhealthy to sleep without a window open."

"Is that another scientific fact?" Sandy said.

"Talk about shorts," I said.

"Why? What's the matter?" David asked, and looked down at himself.

"Are those silk?" Sandy said.

"No, they're cotton and dacron. What's the matter with them?"

"Very sexy," I said.

"They look like silk," Sandy said.

"They're just plain undershorts," David said.

"Just your regular garden variety undershorts," Sandy said.

"I also like the color," I said. "What color is that, David?"

"Blue."

"Looks more like turquoise to me," Sandy said.

Mincing, David put one hand on his hip, sashayed across the room, said, "*I* think they're *adorable* shorts," and then took them off and tossed them over the lampshade.

"Positively cunning little shorts," Sandy said.

"Listen," David said, "I can't open this window until I get my pajamas."

"Why don't you sleep in your cunning little shorts?" Sandy said.

"Peter, go get my pajamas, will you?"

"Go get your own pajamas."

"How can I? I'm naked."

"Give him a robe, Sandy."

"There's one in the closet."

"It won't fit me," David said.

"So go to bed and shut up," I said.

"Will you open the window?"

"I'll open the window."

"*After* I'm in bed."

"After, after," I said.

"Okay," David said, and pulled back the covers, and got into bed, and then tucked quilt and sheet up under his chin.

"Need your teddy?" Sandy asked, and took off her slacks, and went to the closet for a hanger. She folded the slacks carefully, draped them over the bar of the hanger, and was putting them into the closet when David said, "Close the door."

"What?" she said, turning.

"The closet door," David said.

"I think he *does* need his teddy," Sandy said, and closed the door.

"Don't want to let all them hairy things out of the closet," I said.

"I just like the closet door closed," David said.

"Closet door closed, window open," I said, and went to the window and pulled it down about two inches from the top. "Anything else, sir?"

Sandy took off her panties, idly scratched her crotch, looked around the room as though trying to decide whether she'd forgotten anything, and then crossed to the bed and climbed in beside David.

"Anybody remember to put out the cat?" I asked, and took off my shirt.

"Note for the milkman?" David said.

"Porch light on for the kids?"

I hung the shirt over the straight-backed chair at the desk, and then took off my pants and undershorts. "It's too cold in here with that window open," I said.

"Leave it open!" David warned.

"Get the bathroom light," Sandy said.

I went into the bathroom, turned off the light, decided I was thirsty, turned on the light again, and ran a cold glass of water from the sink faucet. "Anybody want water?" I asked.

"Milk and cookies," David said.

I turned out the bathroom light, walked to the floor lamp where David had hung his adorable cunning turquoise shorts, turned that out as well, and then stumbled in the dark toward the bed, climbing in on the other side of Sandy.

"Mmm," Sandy said.

"First time I've felt relaxed all damn day," David said, and sighed.

"Careful," Sandy told him. "That's where the bruise is."

"Here?"

"Mmm. Yes. Be careful."

"How'd you get that, anyway?" I asked.

"I don't know."

"You didn't take any falls, did you?"

"One. But I landed on my hip."

"You think Seymour can manage the north face?"

"Hell with Seymour," David said.

"Hell with them all," Sandy said.

Now entertain conjecture of a time when creeping murmur and the poring dark fills the wide vessel of the universe. From camp to camp, through the foul womb of night, twin

mercenaries skulk in quest of spoils on each small hill. Rose-
buds blatantly explode beneath our stealthy finger treads. (It
is sore, she whispers; gently, it is sore.) Soaring purple columns
rise on either of her flanks; she climbs these spires with her
hands, descends again, besieges and encircles them. Relent-
lessly she strokes with counterpoint precision, urging surrender, promising release, till sudden knowledge of pleasure post-
poned invites her to abrupt cessation. The wind rides hoarsely
in, piercing the night's dull ear, assaulting the now-abandoned
field. So recently addressed, so hotly pressed to yield our
hoarded lodes, we stand in blind rigidity and search the un-
receptive dark, eager for engagement. Between us on the plain
below, spread indifferently and loose, a passive white and
golden mass invites our plunder. In tandem spearhead, we
storm the waiting weald. Fire answers fire, and through the
paly flames all metaphor expires. Now are military allusions
consumed in triple holocaust. In the dark, in the silence, we
play out our sextina.

It is David who presses lips to lips. Much lower, my hand
explores her tangled isosceles. Her back arching, her crotch
to David, buttocks to me, she opens all interiors. Mouth and
vault are wet seducers, crying mutely to the blood.

For now, we are partners. It is *my* blood that echoes the
pulse of her nether lips, stiffens and engorges me. She is wet
at my urging alone. David's tangled hold on her mouth, jaw
gripped, only opens her to new exploration of her crotch.

It is here, at this tempestuous crotch, that Sandy reaffirms
the secret blood oath we took five summers past, and opens
wide remembrance, while promising lips swear allegiance to
David and tangled memories twist on tortured sheets grown
wet.

She turns her face to me, her mouth still wet with David's
kisses, my hand on her crotch where David stiffly probes. His

thrust tangled in my fingers, I can feel the wild blood coursing through his gliding flesh. Her lips strike winter dead. The sun's hot eye opens.

Acrobatically, she twists and opens her thighs to accept me from behind. Wet, unresistant, she proffers me her lips and I plunge deep inside her tilted crotch. David waits for her, stiff with his own blood. She lowers her mouth, hair and teeth tangled.

Our triple alliance is tangled, tender and fierce, gently cruel. It opens for us wide viaducts through which the blood can secretly flow, red and rich and wet. It joins us irrevocably—one crotch, one male member, one pair of thirsting lips.

Anonymous lips hopelessly tangled, Sandy's crotch seems mine (or his) that opens. Wet confusion comes at last— thick as blood.

Spectator sports bore me to death.

Rising at the crack of dawn, the Valley instructors had laid out a slalom course on the slope immediately facing Semanee Lodge, flag-marked poles zigzagging down the left-hand side of the hill, the rest of the slope left open for those skiers indifferent to the thrills of outdoor competition. We decided to watch the race only because at breakfast we'd learned the big cats were still up on the north face, packing the trails, and that most of them would not be opened till midmorning. The race was scheduled to begin at ten o'clock. We finished breakfast at about twenty to, by which time a sizable crowd, buzzing and laughing and chanting slogans, had gathered at the base of the slope. The day was mild and cloudless, with hardly any wind. Foderman, excited and flushed, found a place for us close to the finish line, and said he was anticipating the race with great relish (hold the mustard and sauerkraut, please). We took off our parkas, sat on them, and watched one small

Snowclad contingent as it draped a hand-lettered "Get Semanee!" banner over the entrance to the chair lift, unfazed by the heckling of Semanee supporters below. Face tilted to the sun, Sandy munched on a Baby Ruth (after having consumed four eggs and six slices of toast at breakfast). The smell of chocolate hovered on the air.

At ten minutes to ten, Hollis ambled over. He was wearing one of those white cloth markers they give racing contestants, looped and tied over the arms and shoulders, the black numeral "7" emblazoned across his chest. Taffy was following along behind him like a puppy who'd been taught a few new tricks.

"Hey, howdy," Hollis said. "How's the king of the mountain this morning?"

"Fine, thank you," Foderman said.

"You guys should've come with us last night," Taffy said. "We had a ball."

"Sure did," Hollis said, and smiled down at her. "Anybody see Mary Margaret around?"

"Nope," Sandy said, and took another bite of her Baby Ruth.

"Are you in the race?" Foderman asked.

"Well, that's what the number's for, Seymour," Hollis said.

"We'll be rooting for you," David said drily.

"I sure hope he wins," Taffy said.

"Mm," I said.

"I better get up there," Hollis said. "I'll see you later." He took Taffy's hand, and they both walked briskly toward the chair lift.

"Sweet couple," David said.

"Love him, loathe her," Sandy said.

"He'd better be careful," Foderman said, shaking his head. "She's just a child."

It occurred to me that Rhoda had been at least as much a child that summer five years ago. I closed my eyes. The sun hot on my face, the scent of chocolate in my nostrils, the buzz of conversation swarming, hazily I thought of Rhoda. Poor Rhoda. Conscience of the world. I remembered her telling me once that she always had the feeling there was a party in progress to which she had not been invited. I did not know what she meant at the time. "The summer my mother died," she had said, "should have been the last summer for me. I should have grown up fast and all at once, I should have come face to face with all the loss anyone ever has to experience. But each year, I seem to lose a little more, more and more each summer, until I want to shout '*Leave* me something, at least please leave me *something*,' until I want to grab a microphone the way I did at Sandy's house, and sing out louder than the noise, and thank everyone for listening, and then smile and tell them who I am, *me*, 'My name is *Rhoda*.' But I know, I know inside it isn't any use, I'll have to lose everything sooner or later, and I'll join the others, yes, I'll huddle with them in fear, and the party'll end the minute I get there. *That'll* be the last summer, Peter. Mine and maybe everybody's. And I'm so afraid of winter coming."

Well, sure. Loss of innocence. I mean, that's what it was all about, wasn't it? Hadn't she been talking about, well, fear of losing her virginity or whatever? I mean, that was it, wasn't it? I mean, *that* much seemed perfectly clear. Or had she been trying to say something else, had I missed something? Join the others, huddle with them in fear, what did that mean? What others? What fear? Were David, Sandy, and I the others? And had it been her fear of *us* that allowed what happened in the forest to happen? But no, you see, because then, you see, I would have to subscribe to Krakauer's theory that we had *raped* Rhoda, that we had *forced* ourselves upon

Rhoda, that what had occurred was without Rhoda's full consent and cooperation. And that would make us, well, *bad* guys, you see. That would make us villains. That would make us, you see, evil.

I am no expert on evil (the *Arabs* are expert on that, according to Foderman), but I can swear on my eyes that we intended no harm to that girl. Whatever happened to Rhoda wasn't the same as deliberately going after somebody with the idea of hurting him, as for example the way Mary Margaret had gone after Foderman last night, with all that Jew stuff, and goading him into taking the hill, and then humiliating him that way. We never did anything like that to Rhoda. We *liked* Rhoda.

"Hello there, Seymour. I hardly recognized you with your pants on."

I opened my eyes and looked up. Mary Margaret, wearing her customary green outfit, had joined the group and was even now unzipping her parka preparatory to spreading it on the ground. "Everybody ready for the north face?" she asked.

"Soon as the race is over," Foderman said, and smiled.

"Maybe you two ought to try it alone," Sandy said.

"Why?" Mary Margaret asked.

"I don't want to be responsible for Seymour."

"Responsible? What do you think'll happen to him?"

"Who knows?" Sandy said. "His pants seem to keep falling around his ankles. That could be very dangerous."

"I'm sure Seymour can keep his pants on. Right, Seymour?"

"Why'd you pull them down last night?" Sandy asked flatly.

"I didn't," Mary Margaret said. "The boys did."

"Sure," Sandy said, and nodded.

"Come on, come on," Foderman said, "it was a joke."

"That's all it was," Mary Margaret said, and patted his knee.

"I guess I have no sense of humor," Sandy said.

"Me, neither," David said.

"Would you have liked it better if those gorillas had thrown him halfway across the valley?"

"You saved Seymour's life, right?" Sandy asked.

"Give her a medal," David said.

"You don't know those three guys as well as I do," Mary Margaret said. "They can get mean as hell."

"But not you, babe, huh?" David said.

"There isn't a mean bone in my body," Mary Margaret said, and smiled.

"Look, stop making a federal case out of it," Foderman said. "There was no harm done. Let's all go skiing together and forget it, okay?"

"Maybe they're afraid of the north face," Mary Margaret said.

"Gee, yeah," Sandy said.

"Terrified," David said.

"If you're *not* afraid . . ."

"Jesus, you're too much," Sandy said.

"Then prove it."

"I think you're missing the point, sweetheart," David said.

"What's the point?"

"We don't mind skiing the north face . . ."

"We just don't want to ski it with *you.*"

"Get it?" David said.

"That's rude," Foderman said.

"Seymour," I said, "what the hell's the matter with you? She made a *fool* of you last night."

"I didn't feel foolish."

"Then you *are* a fool," Sandy said.

"It was a joke. What's everybody getting so excited about?"

"You want to hear my appraisal of the situation?" Mary Margaret asked.

"No, not particularly," Sandy said.

"*I* would like to hear it," Foderman said.

"Good, then hear it," Sandy said, and got to her feet. She picked up her parka, brushed snow from it, put it on, and was zipping it up when Mary Margaret said, "Is that the one you stole?"

"Yep," Sandy said. "Coming, guys?"

"It seems to me," Foderman said, "that you can at least allow her the courtesy . . ."

"No, let her go," Mary Margaret said. "She's afraid, can't you see that?"

"Afraid of what?" Foderman said, bewildered.

"Afraid of *me*."

The two girls were facing each other now, Mary Margaret still sitting on the ground, her face tilted, her eyes squinted against the sun, Sandy looking down at her. The exchange that followed was deadly and dangerous, a bitchy, catlike dialogue that I was sure would end in one of those hair-pulling, rolling-on-the-ground, spitting, biting, clawing contests that were all the vogue in grade-B movies before women began burning their bras and punching each other like mere men.

"Now, why would I be afraid of you?" Sandy asked sweetly. "You're a lovely gentle person . . ."

"I am."

"With beautiful delicate hands . . ."

"Then why don't you like me?"

"Don't force me to be blunt."

"Oh? Were you being subtle until now?"

"Okay, Mary Margaret. I don't like you because you're a sadistic anti-Semite with a perverse sense of humor, okay? I think you're out to hurt Seymour. I don't want to be around when you do it. Now fuck off."

"But that's not why you're afraid of me," Mary Margaret said, and smiled. "Why won't you admit the real reason?"

"You don't listen, do you?"

"I listen. I listen very hard. Why are you afraid of me?"

"I'm not afraid of you."

"Then, why won't you ski with me?"

"I don't like you."

"Why not?"

"For the sake of the deaf, dumb, and blind," Sandy said, "I'll repeat what I said three minutes ago. You're an anti-Semite, you've got a perverse . . ."

"Seymour doesn't think I'm an anti-Semite."

"Seymour wouldn't know an anti-Semite from an Arabian pony."

"We were just kidding around last night. Seymour knows that."

"I don't think you were kidding around."

"Come on, Sandy, it was all a big joke."

"I didn't find it comical."

"Then, maybe you're right. Maybe you haven't got a sense of humor."

"Right, I haven't."

"Except for jokes that originate in your tight little corporation."

"Right. You finished? I don't want to miss the big race."

"Why are you putting down the race? Because you're not in it?"

"David? Peter? Let's go."

"Sure, call your dogs."

"Don't press your luck, Mary."

"It's Mary Margaret."

"Sorry."

"No, you're not. That was another put-down. Get my name

wrong, and you reduce me in importance. *That's* what you're afraid of, Sandy."

"Your name?"

"No. The fact that you can't reduce me in importance. I don't *want* to join your exclusive little country club, and you know it."

"You haven't been invited to join."

"Of course not. There are only three members, and they run the admissions committee. You *can't* let anybody else in, because they're liable to find out you don't have a swimming pool or tennis courts or lockers or anything but mirrors. It's all a trick with mirrors, Sandy."

"Then, why do you want to ski with us?"

"I don't. The truth is *you* want to ski with *me*."

"Sure. You go right on believing that."

"And you're *afraid* to. That's the truth."

"There's nothing on the north face . . ."

"Never mind the north face. We're not talking about Seymour now. You're afraid of *me*, not the mountain. And it isn't because you think I'm going to hurt Seymour. It's because you think I'm going to hurt *you*. I'm going to get inside that phony little club of yours and bust all the mirrors."

"Not a chance," Sandy said.

"Try me," Mary Margaret said, and smiled.

It seemed to me that Sandy had lost the argument. I had never before that moment felt any need to feel sorry for Sandy, but Mary Margaret had just shredded her to ribbons, and I sat on the ground with the sun on my face and looked up at Sandy and knew that if she grabbed for the bait Mary Margaret had just offered, she would only be admitting defeat. I saw this knowledge on Sandy's face as well, and wanted to kiss both her cheeks and hug her close and comfort her. I waited for her answer, knowing what the answer would be, knowing Mary Margaret had left no choice but to accept the challenge, to prove to her for all of us that what we shared was not so fragile as to be shattered by a freckle-faced twirp with pretty hands. Sandy was trapped, we were all trapped; Mary Margaret had forced us into a position the way she had forced Foderman to climb that hill.

"We'll meet you on the summit after the race," Sandy said quietly.

"Fine," Mary Margaret said.

The north face was cold and bleak and forbidding.

We stood on the level stretch of ground to the left of the unloading platform, waiting for Foderman and Mary Margaret to arrive at the summit, cursing the absence of a warming hut, shivering as each new fierce gust of wind blew snow ghosts into our faces. Lulled by the sunshine and balmy breezes on the other side of the mountain, we were unprepared for such a frigid assault, and improperly dressed for it. This was Vermont weather, ten below at the top, frostbite lurking if you stood still for more than a minute. Back East, we'd have worn a woolen shirt and two sweaters over our thermal underwear. We'd have zipped the linings into our parkas, put on wet pants over our regular garden variety ski pants, pulled slitted suede masks over our faces. Here in the glorious West, we trembled in our lightweight parkas, did windmill exercises with our arms, jumped up and down on our skis, blew on our hands, and decided that if Foderman and Mary Margaret did not show within the next two minutes, we were heading down without them. They arrived thirty seconds short of the deadline. The chair ride up had numbed them to the marrow, and we waited another five minutes for them to go through the same warming-up exer-

cises we had just performed, while we grew colder and colder
and more and more irritable.

It is dangerous to ski when you are cold.

Aside from the obvious physical disadvantage of tight muscles and aching toes and fingertips, there is a psychological
disadvantage as well. When the temperature drops below
zero and the wind adds its ferocity to the already biting cold,
there is an urgent need to get down to where it is warmer.
A skier who is cold skis faster than he normally would, takes
reckless chances he would otherwise avoid, all in an attempt
to escape those howling wolves chasing the troika. He knows
only that if he remains where he is, he will freeze solid to the
side of the mountain. So he will run over helpless babes and
mewling kittens in his desperate headlong plunge down the
mountain in search of warmth. None of which excuses Mary
Margaret for deliberately breaking Foderman's leg. She was
cold, we all were cold. But she was an expert skier and could
have avoided the accident.

The north face was everything Hollis had promised.

A full view of the difficult terrain on the chair ride up had
been anything but reassuring. Wide fields of moguls blistered
the sharp descent, each threatening mound looking like a concrete World War II pillbox in a frozen Maginot Line. Connecting links stitched their way brokenly across the face of
the mountain, opened suddenly into icy chutes that plunged
vertically into yet more fields of closely spaced moguls. The
turns were abrupt and narrow, treacherously clinging to cliff
faces so steep they could not hold snow, exposing instead
jagged rock formations that had been thrust up out of the
earth Christ knew how many centuries before. Most of the
trails appeared windblown and glazed with ice, flanked with
deep snow waiting in ambush to catch a tip or an edge. I said
nothing to Sandy on the chair ride up, and I said nothing now

as we prepared to ski down. I was very frightened. I had
stopped worrying about Foderman because I was honestly
more concerned for my own safety. I realized, of course, that
his usual technique simply would not work on this enormously
challenging terrain. But I only thought of this fleetingly. I
was cold, and I was frightened, and I wanted to get down to
the bottom as fast as I could.

Mary Margaret was a superb skier and an excellent guide.
Since she had skied the north face last year, and was familiar
with it, she quite naturally took the lead now, with Sandy close
behind her, Foderman and David next in the formation, and
me in the rear. Foderman, much to my surprise, skied with
caution and control, adapting his bulldozing style to the
exigencies of the situation, forcing himself to make frequent
turns in answer to the demands of the mountain; he *had* to
make the turns, in fact, or he'd have gone off into space and
(as Hollis had put it) never been heard from since. We
started down through a glade of pines through which the trail
deceptively and lazily wound, coming out without warning
onto a wide but extremely steep slope. Mary Margaret sliced
the hill diagonally in an oblique traverse, neutralizing the
fall line, gliding effortlessly down and across the face of the
trail. Following her, it all seemed easy. Even Foderman had
no difficulty, and I was beginning to think we'd make a good
skier out of him before his stay at Semanee ended. Dogging
her tracks, we reached an almost level stretch of ground partially covered with glare ice, skirted easily around the patch,
carved wide turns around the bend in the trail, and came out
onto a narrow passage clinging to the outer edge of the mountain with a drop on the left that fell away vertically to a
jagged rock outcropping below. But Mary Margaret handled
this with ease as well. The tails of her skis thrust partially out
over the edge of the mountain, tips angled toward the wall

of snow on her right, checking enough to control her speed but not enough to turn her or to stop her, she led us safely over the ridge and around a curve that opened onto the first wide field of moguls.

We were beginning to warm up a little, but none of us was eager to stop and bask in the sun, not with that wind still raging in over the top of each rounded mogul. Like mist rising over a fen, the snow shifted and swirled as Mary Margaret in green led the way down, again cutting the mountain in a gliding traverse, turning, traversing to the left, turning again, endlessly repeating the pattern until we reached a section of the trail protected from the wind by a gigantic spruce forest. We stopped there to catch our breath. I glanced into the forest. It was shaded and still.

"How we doing?" Mary Margaret asked.

"Good," Foderman said.

"You're a nice skier," she told him. "Everybody else okay?"

"Fine," Sandy said.

"You're all nice skiers," Mary Margaret said, and grinned broadly. There was in her voice a note of condescension, the patronizing tone a master uses to a pupil. Nor had we missed her pointed equation. Foderman was a nice skier, and the three of us were also nice skiers.

"The thing that's gorgeous about this side of the mountain," Mary Margaret said, "is the variety. You never know what's coming up next. You'll see what I mean. It's really exciting."

"I love it so far," Foderman said.

"I knew you would, Seymour."

"I really do love it."

"Don't get carried away, Seymour," David said.

"He's a nice skier," Mary Margaret said.

"Yes, we're *all* nice skiers," Sandy said, letting Mary Margaret know she had caught the earlier appraisal of our skills, and blowing her nose to emphasize the point and to dismiss the slanderous comparison.

"Well, shall we go?" Mary Margaret asked.

The wind, lying in wait just beyond the edge of the forest, leaped across the trail as Mary Margaret led us through a deep crevasse. Walls of snow on either side of us rose to hide the sun, causing the temperature (psychologically at least) to drop another five degrees. I was beginning to understand what she meant about this side of the mountain. There was no way of handicapping it, no way of predicting responses to secrets it stubbornly withheld. There are mountains that become boring the second time down. The skier learns the trails, establishes a rhythm that nullifies their challenge, and then can ski them effortlessly. There was no doing that on the north face. The crevasse became a narrow catwalk that became another field of moguls that became an icy chute that became a shaded glade that became an open, sun-drenched, virtually flat plain. The challenge was continuous, the mountain refused to be second-guessed. I had the feeling it could be skied indefinitely without ever fully revealing its treasures.

We came across one of those tight little ridges Hollis had talked about, where the trail was barely wide enough to permit passage of both skis, and the outside drop was a sheer cliff surely leading to the very bowels of the earth. I navigated that precipitous ledge with dread certainty that I would fall off the mountain and be found below only months later, crushed and broken, when the Ski Patrol swept the trails during the spring thaw. We skied for what seemed forever on that sharply angled ribbon, Foderman hugging the side of the mountain, Sandy standing erect in defiance, I watching my outside ski for fear it would slip off the ledge and send me on my anticipated trip, David doing God knew what behind me. But at last the trail began to widen, and finally it opened onto a field of small, gently rolling hills, the far sides of which sloped gradually to the next small crests beyond. Mary Margaret, as she had done throughout, showed us the way to best enjoy this new terrain. She skied to the top of the nearest hill, jumped, soared six feet through the air with arms akimbo like a big green bird, landed on the downside, glided to the top of the next hill and jumped again, knees bent to absorb the shock as she landed, rising again to take the next crest and the next jump, as free of gravity as though she were on the moon. We leaped from hillock to hillock, exhilarated. It was on the next stretch of trail that Mary Margaret broke Foderman's leg.

He had, until that time, been skiing like an angel, keeping his place in the formation, following not three feet behind the tails of Mary Margaret's skis, fastidiously imitating each of her moves. Exuberantly, he took the jumps with each of us, and then—perhaps because he was so excited, perhaps because he was still cold in spite of all the leaping—regressed to his earlier downhill technique, and schussed the remainder of the field, passing Mary Margaret, taking the lead, and disappearing from sight around a bend at the bottom. Mary Margaret was immediately behind him, and I was behind her. I saw everything that happened. The mountain, in another of its surprises, unraveled a rather steep twisting trail some four feet wide, running through a V-like crotch bounded on both sides by angled walls of snow. Foderman, who should have known by this time that the mountain was secretive and perverse, went into the trail as if it were a continuation of the gently rolling field we had just come down. He was skiing far too fast, and was not skillful enough to check his speed in such a narrow passage. A simple snowplow check would not have worked here because he'd have had to apply pressure by bending sharply at the knees, tips pointed toward each other, and the spread heels of his skis would have struck the walls on either side of the trail, resulting in a certain fall. A better skier would have slowed himself by executing a series of short, sharp heel thrusts, exactly as Mary Margaret and I were doing. If Foderman had been behind either of us, he might have followed our example, imitated our moves, and been able to ski the passage with ease. But he was in the lead, and clearly at a loss, gaining momentum and speed, and faced with a sharp turn below which he could not possibly negotiate if he did not somehow slow down.

He resorted to a beginner's device. He sat abruptly, his fat backside thudding into the snow. Sliding down the trail on his back, knees bent, skis flat on the ground, arms and poles up and away from his body, he might have been fine if his right ski hadn't suddenly darted out from under him, the leg shooting straight up into the air. He slipped sideways across the trail, and the heel of the right ski came down hard, sinking deep into the soft snow adjacent to the sloping wall. He was now athwart the trail, head and shoulders against the left wall, elbows bent, left knee bent and left ski flat on the ground, right leg extended straight with the tail of the right ski anchored firmly in the snow. He looked rather like a railroad crossing, his leg effectively barricading the trail, his boot fastened to the ski. I suddenly remembered that Sandy had tightened the binding on that ski only two days ago, and I wondered if Foderman had since had it readjusted.

It was too late.

Mary Margaret was skiing toward him.

There were several things Mary Margaret could have done. She was an expert skier. She had been checking her speed all the way down the trail, and most certainly could have executed a stop now. Or she could have jumped *over* the barricade of Foderman's leg; his foot, firmly bound to the ski, was no more than three feet off the ground. But she lowered her head in-

stead, bent her knees, crouched into a downhill schuss position, and raced directly for Foderman where he lay helplessly
pinioned athwart the trail. A moment before she crashed into
his leg, I realized she was determined to ski *through* him.

His scream echoed off the walls of the narrow canyon. The
force of their collision sent Mary Margaret into a somersault-
ing roll over Foderman's body. Thrashing, flailing, she went
skidding down the trail while Foderman lay screaming in
agony, the splintered bones of his leg showing through the
torn ski pants. He was still screaming when she rolled to a stop
some twelve feet below him, unharmed.

Every Saturday night, at alternating hotels in the Valley,
the Semanee ski instructors awarded bronze or silver pins to
those of their pupils who had made the most progress during
the preceding week. On this Saturday, the ceremony—further
enhanced by presentation of bronze, silver, and gold medals
to winners of the big race that morning—was to be held at
Semanee Lodge, shortly after dinner.

The Lodge, I must say, had been decorated resplendently
for the occasion and for the imminent holiday only two days
off. While most of the guests were out skiing that afternoon
(and while at least one of them was having his leg broken),
the hotel staff had decked the halls with boughs of holly and
had erected (you should pardon the expression) a giant
Christmas tree in the lobby, glistening with pinpoints of light
and hung with tinsel and balls (you should again pardon the
expression). The mood was festive and gay as skiers from all
over the Valley gathered in the large lounge to reward those
among them who had performed admirably. Sandy, David,
and I were depressed.

We had accompanied Foderman to the hospital, where we
were informed by the resident orthopedist, a man who treated

hundreds of ski injuries each season, that Foderman had suf-
fered a highly comminuted, compound fracture of the tibia
and fibula, none of which meant a damn thing to us until he
explained it. Solemnly and dispassionately, the doctor said that
the bones in Foderman's right leg had been splintered into too
many pieces to allow internal repair by operation. He would
have to debride the skin wound, close it up, feed Foderman
antibiotics intravenously (we were lucky to be on the scene,
the doctor told us, because if there had been too long a delay
in getting Foderman to a hospital, overwhelming infection
and eventual loss of the leg would have been distinct possibilities), and put him in skeletal traction for some eight to
twelve weeks, after which time he would be wearing a cast
for anywhere from twenty-four to twenty-six weeks. In short,
it was bad.

Leaving Foderman under heavy sedation, we had walked
back to the Lodge with Mary Margaret, who tearfully insisted
the accident was unavoidable. We told her exactly what we
thought about *that* little piece of expiation, and removed
ourselves from her presence the moment we got to the hotel.
Now, as Hans Bittner checked out the microphone ("Vun,
two, tree, testing") and the band began setting up in the
corner of the room where the awards were to be presented, I
found myself thinking about Mary Margaret and wondering
why she had deliberately crashed into Foderman's extended
leg.

It seemed to me there were only three possibilities worth
consideration. The first of these was the undeniable fact that
Mary Margaret was a bigot. Nor did it surprise me that a member of one much-maligned minority group should be able to
hate a member of another minority group. When it came to
hating Jews, for example, there was no one who did it as pas-
sionately as the black man. Ah yes, but couldn't I maintain

that Mary Margaret had risen above all that? Couldn't I say
that here in this wonderful land of opportunity for all, regard-
less of race, creed, color (or anything but the accidental
beauty of a person's hands), Mary Margaret had been able
to break through the cultural restrictions placed upon her
crazy immigrant father, was now coining money hand over
fist (so to speak), and therefore could afford to be more
generous in spirit toward those less-fortunate minority-group
members who were still merely gynecologists? I could say that,
but I wouldn't believe it for a minute. Mary Margaret hated
Jews, and for all her buttering up of Foderman ("You're my
date, Seymour," and "I knew you'd love it, Seymour"), she
was entirely capable of turning him into a lampshade or a bar
of soap at the drop of a yarmulke. Okay. So she had broken
his leg because she hated Jews. Nothing personal, you understand. She had nothing against dear old Dr. Seymour Foderman that she didn't have against any and all Jews. Foderman
just happened to be handy when the moment came to exorcise
that hatred. So *splat* went Foderman's leg, "Oh my, I'm *so*
sorry, I just couldn't avoid the accident. He was sprawled
all across the trail there, you know, I couldn't turn, I couldn't
jump, I couldn't stop, I simply *had* to run right through him.
Can't you see how distressed I am? Look at me. Can't you see
I'm crying?"

That was the first possibility.

The second possibility was something darker to think about,
and it had nothing to do with prejudice. It had only to do with
evil. There is evil, and there is evil; as Foderman pointed out,
there is a vast difference between the death and the fever. It
is one thing to be an Archie Bunker type mouthing adorable
racial and ethnic slurs in a lovable guy-next-door fashion, but
it's quite another thing to be mean as cat shit, and to shatter

someone's leg merely because he happens to be a Jew. *That,* man, is evil. *That* is the death as compared to the fever.

I often sense when talking to Dr. Krakauer that he somehow feels Sandy, David, and I are evil. He's never come out and said so in as many words, but a man who insists we committed rape would *have* to believe we're evil unless he also believes rape is just another innocent American pastime. I won't go into the long session (it seemed long) that Crackers and I had just before my departure for Semanee, but he said during that interminable fifty minutes that whatever the three of us shared was unhealthy at best and evil at worst. He didn't say evil exactly. But he certainly intimated it. (Or perhaps not. Analysts aren't supposed to make value judgments.) But he did say a lot about narcissism and about being able to excuse whatever ternary acts we performed because we enjoyed, in effect, the approval of the peer group, which peer group wasn't that at all but merely a three-way reflecting mirror so that in reality we were enjoying only *self*-approval. He went on to say (dig this) that our relationship was a form of *non*-relating, and that we clung to each other so desperately because we were incapable of relating to *anyone*, least of all ourselves. In other words (and I repeat all this bullshit only to make a point about Mary Margaret), the highly personal relationship we *thought* we shared was really entirely *im*personal.

But if Crackers really *did* believe we were evil, how did he account for the fact that none of us felt an iota of guilt about what we had done together with Rhoda? (Spare me a lengthy dissertation about the psychopathic personality, okay, Doc?) The truth was we did *not* feel guilty, we had done nothing to feel guilty *about*. Mary Margaret, on the other hand, had wept all the way from the hospital, and what were her tears if not an open admission that she had done something terrible, something unspeakably horrible, something in fact evil? She was crying because she felt guilty. And she felt guilty because not only was she a bigot, she was an *evil* bigot to boot.

Or (and this was the third and darkest possibility of all) perhaps she had broken Foderman's leg in a misguided effort to please us. The three of us. Sandy, David, and me. I realized, even as I thought of it, that if I ever mentioned the idea to Crackers he would use it as evidence against me. He would say I was only trying to glorify the friendship by setting it above and apart from the puny, meaningless relationships other humans shared, thereby isolating us further from the peasants and enabling us to withdraw more completely into ourselves—which of course meant withdrawing more completely into a *single* self, narcissism again, ho-hum.

But *wasn't* it a possibility? Mary Margaret had mistakenly believed from the very start that we were actively engaged in trying to break Foderman's leg. Admiring our style, desirous of getting into our closed circle, wasn't it entirely possible she had broken Foderman's leg in an attempt to ingratiate herself with us? Like a cat bringing home dead chipmunks and laying them on the doormat? Had breaking Foderman's leg been her way of meeting initiation requirements? Had she erroneously and crazily assumed we would *applaud* such a terrible deed?

The idea amused me.

It also frightened me.

It frightened me that it amused me.

Was I, in fact (and this was what annoyed me most about analysis), *pleased* that Mary Margaret had gone to such lengths to engage our attention, court our approval, and be accepted into our tight society? Was I *really* shocked and angry, or was I secretly delighted? Jesus, I thought. If I'm *glad* she broke his leg, then maybe we *intended* to break it all along. ("Vun, two, tree, testing," Bittner said again.)

No.

We were not culpable. It was all right to consider Mary Margaret an amoral bitch, but it was all wrong to believe we had in any way encouraged her behavior. We simply had not. Sandy had told her frankly, bluntly, and perhaps cruelly, that we considered her a sadistic Jew-hater. We had made it plain we did not like her, we had told her we did not want to ski with her, and we had accompanied her this morning only to make certain she would not try to harm Foderman. Yes, Mary Margaret was the death, all right, Mary Margaret was that hairy stinking thing Foderman had described. But we were not about to be accepted as the fever, thank you. We were not about to think of ourselves as motivating forces, begging forgiveness as the lesser of two evils. Our temperature was 98.6, quite normal.

"Ladies and gentlemen," Bittner said, "we are so happy tonight to make the awards from our instructors for those skiers who have achieved according to their merits the most advances in their classes on the slopes this week."

"Mind if we join you?" Penn Trate asked.

"All the tables seem to be full," Mrs. Trate said.

"Sure, sit down," David said unenthusiastically.

"And, at the end, when we are finally giving out all the pins," Bittner said, "we will have the extreme honor of presenting to the winners of the race this morning for the slalom, the honor of the Semanee bronze, silver, and gold medals."

"I don't believe we've formally met," Trate said. "I'm John Hennings, and this is my wife Matilda."

"Tish," she said, and smiled.

"Her nickname," Trate said, and smiled.

"Sandy."

"David."

"Peter," I said.

"I understand your friend had an accident," Trate said. "Honey, do you want something to drink?"

"Yes, a little crème de menthe, please," Tish said.

"Racked himself up pretty bad, from what I hear," Trate said.

"Johnny, let's not talk about ski accidents," Tish said. "I get very nervous."

"Tish is a beginner," Trate said.

"He'll be in traction for eight weeks," Sandy said.

"So now," Bittner said into the microphone, and winced as feedback pierced the air. Moving away from the mike, he said, "What the hell is that, huh?" and smiled at the audience. Max fiddled with the amplifier, and then Bittner came back to the mike and said again, "So now . . . ahhh, that's better . . . so now, without further announcement, we will have presenting the awards for the Beginners' classes, that's groups 6A and 6B, Mr. Martin Hirsch, who you perhaps all know as the Silver Streak. Martin?"

Accompanied by a flourish from the band, Hirsch, gray-haired and suntanned, came up to the microphone and joylessly read off the names of the bronze and silver pin recipients. The skiers approached the bandstand like winners of the Academy Award, beaming at their friends, waving to well-wishers in the crowd. I fully expected them to make acceptance speeches in which they thanked their agents, their acting coaches, their hairdressers, and their trusty police dogs. Instead, clutching their coveted prizes, they walked proudly back to their tables, while the band played another brief flourish and the ski instructors stood and grinned along the wall.

"Hello, folks, would you care for something to drink?" Alice asked.

"Yes, a crème de menthe, please," Trate said, "and I'll . . ."

"On the rocks or straight up?"

"Straight up," Tish said, and I could tell from the faint flush on her cheeks that she considered this somehow suggestive.

"And you, sir?" Alice asked. "Hi, Peter."

"Hi, Alice."

"I'll have a Martini, very dry, with Beefeater's gin and a twist of lemon," Trate said.

"You busy later?" Alice asked me.

"Why?"

"Like to talk to you," she said.

"Did you get that, miss?"

"I got it," Alice said. "Okay?" she said to me.

"Fine," I said.

"Anybody else?" Alice asked.

"Beer for me," Sandy said.

"Beer all around," David said.

"Shall I bring a pitcher?"

"Great."

"I'm off at midnight," Alice said, and moved swiftly away from the table.

"She's awfully cute," Tish said.

"Mmm," I said.

"How'd your friend happen to hurt himself?" Trate asked.

"*Please*, Johnny," Tish said.

"I'm just curious, honey."

"Well, they can tell you about it later. Honestly, I've never met anyone so morbidly interested in ski accidents."

"Builds my confidence, honey," he said, and grinned.

"Now," Bittner said at the microphone, "to present the awards for the classes 5A and 5B, we have someone you probably know best as the star violinist in our trio here at the Lodge, but who also instructs on the slopes in his spare time, Mr. Max Brandstaetter."

Max took the microphone with professional aplomb and

read off the names of the bronze and silver pin winners. Alice came back with the drinks. Leaning over me as she put them down on the table, she whispered, "Don't forget."

"I won't."

"Promise?"

"I promise," I said, and watched her swiveling off in dirndl and peasant blouse.

"She's awfully cute," Tish said.

The awards went on interminably. Max, finished with his presentation stint, wandered over to our table, and took a chair alongside David. At Trate's insistence, I told him about Foderman's accident. Max asked David if he would care to play with the band again tonight. Sandy stared off into space as the pins were awarded to 3A and 3B. It was precisely at this point that Mary Margaret arrived.

It must have taken considerable courage for her to cross that room and join us at the table as though nothing had happened to our social contract. We had condemned her bitterly on the walk from the hospital, had bluntly told her she'd be lucky if we didn't inform the local constabulary that she had flagrantly committed armed assault on a helpless victim, to which she had tearfully countered, "And suppose I tell about the parka?" to which Sandy had replied, "Shoplifting ain't mugging in the park," and Mary Margaret had blown her nose and said, "I keep telling you it was an *accident!*" and Sandy said, "You broke his goddamn leg!" and Mary Margaret said, "I couldn't help it."

So here she was.

"Hey, hi," she said, pulling up a chair alongside Tish. "I don't believe we've met. I'm Mary Margaret Buono."

"Means 'good' in Italian," David said drily.

"I'm John Hennings," Trate said, "and this is my wife Matilda."

"Tish."

"Her nickname," Trate said, and smiled.

"I have a cousin named Matilda," Mary Margaret said. "What's everybody drinking?"

I noticed at once that she was flaunting her hands. She had put on a black, long-sleeved dress that served as a perfect backdrop for those exquisite white hands, and she used them now with supreme confidence that they were stars in a command performance—single hot spotlight, black curtain, introductory drum roll, and "Heeeeeerrrre they *are,* folks!" She had dressed deliberately for the occasion, I was sure, hoping we would be so entranced by the beauty of her hands that we would forget the ugliness of her spirit. Trate was captivated at once. Her hands came out of their basket like twin white cobras, and Trate watched hypnotically. Tish, secure in the allure of her own twin assets (ripely and bra-lessly contained in a scoop-necked halter top that looked like the undershirt Sonny Corleone wore in *The Godfather*), hardly considered a pair of hands competition, and went babbling on to David and Max about how nice it was to be spending the Christmas holidays far from the commercial hustle and bustle of a big town like Portland, Oregon. David made no comment. Max did not know Portland, Oregon from Portsmouth, Virginia.

Sandy totally ignored Mary Margaret; as far as she was concerned, Mary Margaret was already dead. Blue eyes vacant, full mouth drawn tight, blond head erect, she disdainfully consigned Mary Margaret to that great big cemetery in the sky without so much as shedding an obligatory tear over her untimely demise. It was perhaps Sandy's deliberate and premature burial that provoked the next attack from Mary Margaret. I am sometimes quite stupid when it comes to understanding attacks. I seem always to be guarding my front while a pincers assault is being mounted on both flanks. I thought at first that Mary Margaret's attempt to control the conversational flow merely supported my earlier theory—she was somehow trying to *impress* us by exposing the least desirable aspects of her personality. I realized only later that I was deluding myself. However flattering and appealing the idea initially seemed, I became more and more convinced that Mary Margaret was motivated not by admiration but by envy. Which is why I'd been afraid of her from the very beginning. Mary Margaret was out to destroy us.

I do not mean that literally. I do not mean that she entertained actual thoughts of poisoning our drinks or slitting our throats while we slept. She wanted only to destroy our triple identity. (It occurred to me that in many respects she was quite similar to Dr. Krakauer, who in our last session had seemed hell-bent on forcing me into a denial of Sandy and David. I honestly don't know why people are so envious of our unity.) Listening to Mary Margaret as first she flailed out at Max, and then took on the Trates, and then closed the pincers to reveal her true target, I became certain that she was jealous of what we shared, furious that we would not allow her to join us or to separate us, and determined to get inside our phony little club and bust all the mirrors.

She started by drawing out Trate, who, as it developed, was not a corporation executive but a teacher in a small private school on the outskirts of Portland. Trate, flattered to think that anyone could be even slightly interested in the care and feeding of pubescent boys, launched into a learned (and boring) treatise comparing private-school to public-school education, reaching the conclusion (surprise!) that private schools were in every way superior to public schools, which was why he had devoted his life to teaching fine young boys in a healthy, challenging environment, God bless America, pass the apple pie, and for God's sake don't mention busing.

"Yes, but what about homosexuality?" Mary Margaret asked.

"What about it?" Trate said.

"Isn't it rampant?" Mary Margaret asked.

"Where? Do you mean in America?"

"No, I mean in private schools."

"Oh, really," Tish said.

"That's a common misconception," Trate said.

"That little boys are constantly being buggered in private schools?" Mary Margaret said.

"Now, *really*," Tish said.

"We don't have that problem in my school," Trate said.

"Is it a sleep-away school?"

"It's a boarding school, yes."

"Then, how do you avoid the problem?"

"It simply doesn't exist."

"Do you believe that, Max?" Mary Margaret asked.

Max, turning away from his conversation with David, smiled and said, "I beg your pardon, I wasn't listening."

"We were discussing homosexuality," Mary Margaret said.

"Ah, yes? What about it?" Max said.

"Do you have private schools in Europe?"

"Yes?" Max said, puzzled.

"Did you go to a private school when you were a boy?"

"No."

"Then, I suppose you wouldn't know anything about homosexual relationships between little boys," she said, and looked Max square in the eye. To Max's credit, he did not turn away.

"No," he said, "I would know nothing about it."

"There *are* homosexuals in Austria, of course."

"There are," Max said unflinchingly, "homosexuals everywhere."

"My God, how'd we get into *this?*" Tish asked.

"I suppose it's accepted more easily in Europe, though," Mary Margaret said.

"I wish I knew where you'd picked up that idea," Trate said. "I mean, about private schools in America."

"From association with any number of pansies in New York City," Mary Margaret said flatly, "all of whom had been exposed to homosexuality at very early ages in posh little private schools."

"Well, in the East maybe," Trate said.

"The intellectual East," Mary Margaret said.

"I can only speak for my part of the country . . ."

"Where homosexuality is unheard of, right?"

"Listen, you're rather rude, do you know that?" Tish said earnestly.

"I don't mean to be," Mary Margaret said, and smiled pleasantly, and opened her gorgeous hands in a fluid gesture that begged understanding. "I'm really interested in the topic. I'm sure Max is, too."

"I am interested only in skiing," Max said, and smiled, and shrugged.

"Well, you can't ski at night," Mary Margaret said.

Trate glanced sidelong and uneasily at Max, suddenly understanding Mary Margaret's implication. Then, ashamed of his reaction, he quickly said, "Anyway, we're not talking about sex between consenting adults in the privacy of their own . . ."

"I don't know how we got on sex," Tish said, and shook her head.

"We're talking about, well, corrupting *kids.* Isn't that what we're talking about?"

"Who knows?" Mary Margaret said, smiling. "What are we talking about, Max?"

"*I* was talking to David," Max said.

"What about?"

"As I said, skiing."

"Max and I are old friends," Mary Margaret said. "We skied a lot together last year."

"Mary Margaret is a superb skier," Max said generously.

"Are you an instructor, too?" Trate asked her.

"No, no," Mary Margaret said.

"Mary Margaret is a model," Max said. "Show them your beautiful hands, Mary Margaret."

"A model? Really?" Tish said, suddenly interested, and immediately forgetting how rude she had thought Mary Margaret was.

"Her hands," Max said.

"Why, of course!" Tish said. "They're exquisite!"

"What do *you* do, Tish?" Mary Margaret asked, modestly turning attention from her own brilliant career and graciously bowing Tish into stage center.

"Me? I'm just a housewife," Tish answered. "Do you do television commercials and everything?"

"Yes, everything," Mary Margaret said in dismissal. "What do you mean, *just* a housewife? Lots of women's libbers would take offense at that statement, you know."

"Well, it's what I *am*," Tish said, and giggled.

"She's a lot more than just a housewife," Trate said, smiling approval.

"And now," Bittner said at the microphone, "with your kind indulgence, I will read off the names of those contestants who placed in the top ten positions in the slalom, and end finally with the bronze, silver, and gold medal winners in the third, second, and first places. In the tenth position, Mr. Harry Fielder of New York City . . ."

Harry Fielder of New York City, beaming modestly, rose in place at his table and acknowledged the applause of the crowd and the extended paradiddles Helmut played on his snare drum.

"In ninth position, Mr. Hollis Blake from San Manuel, Arizona."

"That's Hollis," Mary Margaret said.

"Hooray for Hollis," David said.

"Nothing wrong with being a housewife," Trate said, as Bittner tediously read the names of runners-up, and Helmut inventively unraveled a series of snare-drum rolls and the instructors grinned and shifted their feet. "Actually, Tish is quite active in . . ."

"Bed," Mary Margaret said immediately, and Max burst out laughing.

"Well, there, too," Trate said awkwardly. "But I meant to say she's quite active in the social life of the school . . ."

"Has all the boys in for tea and sympathy, I'll bet," Mary Margaret said.

"Well, tea, anyway," Trate said.

"No sympathy?"

"She's very understanding of their problems."

"And will they speak kindly of her in later years?" Mary Margaret asked.

"I don't know what you mean."

"*You* know what I mean, don't you, Tish?"

"No, I don't," Tish said, totally bewildered.

"Comfort," Mary Margaret said. "Solace."

"Oh, yes, certainly," Trate said.

"Moral guidance."

"Certainly," Trate said.

"Right, Sandy?"

"What?" Sandy said, surprised she'd been addressed.

"Comfort and solace. For the boys. Isn't that what a good friend should offer them? Moral guidance?" And here she spread her expressive hands wide in a gesture that unmistak-ably indentified David and me as the boys she was talking about.

"And now," Bittner said at the microphone, "we come to those skiers who from all over Semanee Valley and also from all over Snowclad where they came down from there to com-pete, those skiers who finished third, second, and first in that order and who it gives me great pleasure now to introduce their names and to award to them the bronze, the silver, and the gold medals. In other words, ladies and gentlemen, I give you now the three big winners."

In other words, ladies and gentlemen, it was time to quit badgering the likes of Max and the Trates, time to quit wasting time with the also-rans. Instead, Mary Margaret had intro-duced the three big winners (namely yours truly and associates) and was now ready to award the bronze, the silver, and the gold artillery shells. A single glance from Trate informed me that Mary Margaret's opening barrage had been on target. Belatedly, Trate understood the tea and sympathy reference, and realized Mary Margaret had been suggesting that his good wife Matilda the Tish was spending those long wintry campus afternoons doling out more than motherly comfort and solace while he was correcting term papers in the library, was in fact reassuring buggered little boys of their masculinity, guiding them morally by allowing them entrance to the sacred hidden storeroom and permitting them to gaze upon and fondle the Trate treasures, all in a good cause.

His sidelong glance was directed not accusingly at his be-loved faithful wife, but wonderingly at *me*, a glance of the same species and genus he had earlier squandered on Max. He *knew* his precious blushing bride was above suspicion, and could therefore dismiss Mary Margaret's campus fantasy as pure and simple nonsense. But he knew nothing at all about

David or me, having first made our acquaintance this evening, and Mary Margaret had just referred to us as "the boys," time-honored euphemism (even in Portland, Oregon) for pansy, fruit, or queer, and had broadly intimated that Sandy gave to us the comfort, solace, and moral guidance provided at certain exclusive private schools in the East, where white-sneakered, light-footed, limp-wristed students were in constant need of open-bloused bolstering of their male egos, schools where god-damn little fairies, in short, fooled around with the goddamn English teacher's wife while he was out coaching the goddamn track team! Suspicion ran riot. First Max, now David and me! Trate must have felt suddenly surrounded by three flitting fag-gots. David bridled at once. If he had been carrying his flute, I was certain he would have rammed it down Mary Margaret's throat, thereby exacting at least some measure of ironic justice, the punishment fitting the accusation, so to speak. But Sandy surprised me by bursting into explosive laughter, that clever, lovely, marvelous, darling girl.

"In third place, for the honored bronze medal," Bittner said, "I happily announce Mr. Jonas Whelan of Austin, Texas."

"I just thought of something funny," Sandy said.

"Really? What?" Trate asked, eager to get away from a sub-ject that was becoming more disturbing by the minute. The crowd applauded as Mr. Jonas Whelan went up to the band-stand to accept his medal. Sandy's laughter trailed, and a radiant smile replaced it.

"Mary Margaret would appreciate this," she said, and her voice held all the intimate promise of someone about to reveal a cherished secret to a dear and trusted friend. Hans Bittner, grinning, said, "In second place, for the silver medal, I am happy to call to the microphone, Mr. Andrew D'Allesandro of Yonkers, New York." There was more applause as Mr. D'Allesandro shuffled modestly to the bandstand.

"This happened the summer before I met the boys," Sandy said. "I was fourteen at the time."

"I didn't realize you'd known each other that long," Mary Margaret said. Her initial surprise had given way to curiosity. She leaned forward expectantly now, arms on the table, green eyes faintly suspicious.

"Yes, I met them when I was fifteen," Sandy said.

"How old are you now?" Trate asked.

"You're not supposed to ask women their age, Johnny."

"I'm twenty," Sandy said.

"I figured about twenty-two or -three," Trate said.

"Johnny, that's even *worse!*" Tish said.

"What'd I say?" Trate said.

At the microphone, Hans Bittner said, "And now, ladies and gentlemen, it is with great pride that I announce the name of the gold medal winner in today's race, and that is . . ." He hesitated, trying to build suspense, even though everyone had already read the names of the winners on the lobby bulletin board. "Mr. Arthur Greer of Pensacola, Florida. Ladies and gentlemen, Mr. Greer!"

Applause broke out from the crowd as Mr. Greer rose and walked briskly to the bandstand. Sandy waited for the applause to die, and then said, "The summer I was fourteen, my mother and I went up to Martha's Vineyard. We . . ."

"I have been there once," Max said. "It is very nice there."

"Yes, it's lovely," Sandy said.

"I've never heard of it," Trate said.

"We went there because my father had just left after seventeen years of marriage . . ."

"Left?" Tish said.

"Yes. Left my mother."

"Oh, I'm sorry to hear that."

"Well, it was a long time ago."

"Are you an only child?"

"Yes."

"That's not so bad, then."

"My mother has since remarried," Sandy said.

"I'm so happy," Tish said.

"But we were both sort of in shock that summer, and we went up there to get over it."

"You will have to excuse me," Max said. "I think we are ready for some music. David? Join us later, yes?"

"I'll see," David said.

Max clasped him on the shoulder in farewell, and went up to the bandstand, where his fellow musicians were waiting for him. Sandy suddenly laughed again, anticipating her own story, enjoying it in advance.

"Is it *that* funny?" Mary Margaret asked.

"It's pretty funny," Sandy admitted.

"I'm dying to hear it," Trate said.

"Then, keep quiet and let her tell it," Tish said.

"Well, there was a party at our house one night," Sandy said, "and everybody was drinking a lot, and the conversation got around to swimming, and somebody said that women were good endurance swimmers because they had an extra layer of fat on their bodies and could . . ."

"That isn't true," Tish said.

"Yes, it's true, honey," Trate said.

"I don't know whether it's true or not," Sandy said, "but this person was saying that women are supposed to be able to stay in the water longer because of that extra layer of fat."

"*Where'd* you say this happened?" I asked.

"Martha's Vineyard."

"It sounds familiar," David said. "Have you told it before?"

"Maybe," Sandy said, and again laughed. "I don't remember.

The extra layer of fat is supposed to protect women from the cold."

"I could have used an extra layer of fat on the north face today," Trate said.

"Hush, honey."

"So the argument went back and forth and finally someone said, 'Look, Joanna . . .'"

"Who's Joanna?" Trate asked.

"My mother. Someone said, 'Look, Joanna, *you're* a fantastic swimmer, and you haven't got an *ounce* of fat on you, why don't you prove to everybody that it's got nothing to do with *fat*, it's only got to do with women being superior!'"

"We *are* superior," Tish said.

"Quiet, honey."

"*When* did you say this happened?" I asked.

"The summer before we met."

"It still sounds familiar," David said.

It *did* sound familiar. It *was* familiar. I remembered it now, and it wasn't Sandy's story, and it hadn't happened the summer before we'd met, and it wasn't even funny. It was *Rhoda* who'd told it to us one rainy afternoon, and it had happened to her when she was ten, and it was about the night her mother drowned trying to prove to a bunch of drunken idiots that she could swim nonstop to a sand bar half a mile offshore. Puzzled, I looked at Sandy. She laughed again, reassured me with an almost indiscernible nod, and said, "The grown-ups decided to have a race. This must've been about two in the morning, you understand, and most of . . ."

"What were you doing up so late?" Tish asked.

"What?" Sandy said.

"You were only fourteen!" Tish said, shocked.

"Yes, but it was summertime. No school."

"Still," Tish said, and shrugged.

"In fact, there were a *lot* of kids still awake," Sandy said, and I realized she was going to invent this as she went along, using Rhoda's story as a springboard, and leaping off from it into Christ knew what uncharted waters. David suddenly remembered the origin of the story, too, and looked sharply across the table at Sandy, surprised, fascinated and, I was sure, wondering how she hoped to twist an essentially tragic event into something she had already advertised as funny. The suspicion in Mary Margaret's eyes had given way to curiosity. She was genuinely interested in the outcome of the story, eager to know what had happened that night on Martha's Vineyard the summer Sandy was fourteen. *I* was more interested in trying to figure out what Sandy hoped to accomplish. There was no question but that she was winging this directly at Mary Margaret, her eyes, her subdued laughter somehow promising a revelation only the two of them might share. I would have felt enormously neglected if I didn't know Sandy better. She was after something. I watched and listened now as she pursued whatever the hell it was.

"The kids who were still awake ranged in age from twelve to fifteen, and since the grown-ups were . . ."

"That *is* young," Tish said. "Twelve. To be up at two in the morning."

"Quiet, Tish," Trate said.

"Well, it *is*," Tish said.

"Since the grown-ups were about to have a race, we decided to have a race of our own. The idea came from a little girl I despised—a thirteen-year-old whose name I've already forgotten. Iris? Irene? Yes, it was Irene."

As *I* recalled the story, Irene was Rhoda's mother, the woman who had drowned. Sandy seemed to be appropriating characters and plot, loosely reshaping both to suit the needs of a theme she had not yet revealed, a form of borrowing

sometimes known as plagiarism. Apparently, she had decided
to respond peacefully to Mary Margaret's earlier provocation.
If this, then, was an attempt at negotiated settlement, her
story would have to make a point readily understood and accepted by Mary Margaret. Knowing better than to believe
Sandy was in any way retreating, I began wondering how she
could possibly transform tragedy into not only comedy but
comedy that carried the additional burden of peace with
honor. Or was she really seeking peace? As Katherine of France
once remarked, "O bon Dieu! les langues des hommes sont
pleines de tromperies," not to mention the tongues of women,
too.

Fascinated, I listened intently as Sandy described the imaginary little brat named Irene, a girl who sounded very much
like Mary Margaret. (This, then, was to be a parable of sorts.
That long-ago feud twixt Sandy and the invented little monster
was being related to illuminate the existing tension between
Sandy and Mary Margaret.) It seemed that Irene, that darling
little child, had irked Sandy from the beginning of the summer, taunting her, calling her names, embarrassing her in the
presence of other children, once even revealing that Sandy
wore a cotton training bra, how mortifying! On more than one
occasion, surrounded by water as they were, Sandy had considered drowning (source material again) the horrid little
creature, but had put such thoughts out of her mind as being
beyond the capabilities of a mere slip of a fourteen-year-old.
This night of nights, however, seemed to offer splendid opportunity for actually carrying out the foul deed, holding little
Irene's head under water while she gasped her last obscenity
and then sank slowly from sight.

"What do you mean?" Tish asked, alarmed. "You mean you
actually thought of *murdering* her?"

"Drowning her," Sandy said.

"That's murdering her."

"I suppose."

"I've never in my *life* hated a person enough to even *dream* of . . ."

"I was only fourteen," Sandy said.

"Even so."

"Emotions run high at fourteen." She smiled at Mary Margaret. "We learn to control them when we get a bit older. Anyway, let me tell the rest of the story."

"If you're going to say you really *did* drown that little girl . . ."

"No, no, no," Sandy said, and laughed.

"Thank God!"

"She *said* it was a funny story, Tish. Drowning somebody isn't very funny."

"I know, Johnny, but she also said she thought of it. She seriously *considered* it."

"Let me finish, okay?" Sandy said.

"Well, go ahead," Tish said reluctantly.

The band began playing just as Sandy started talking again, a Viennese waltz particularly unsuited to this supposedly hilarious tale she was tortuously unraveling.

"The grown-ups all got into their bathing suits," she said, "and went down to the beach, leaving us kids alone together in the house. Irene began poking me in the belly, and telling the other kids *I* had a layer of fat around *me* . . ."

"What a horrible little child!" Tish said.

"And why didn't we have our *own* little race to prove that I was a lousy swimmer even if I was obese."

"Were you?" Trate asked.

"I was pretty fat that summer. I didn't slim down until the following year. Just before I met the boys."

I didn't know which part of Sandy's story was true and which was false any more, so I merely glanced at David, and he shrugged slightly, and both of us waited for the conclusion to this so-far hysterically funny tale based on an original underwater tragedy by Buster Crabbe.

"Naturally, all the kids thought it would be great fun to do what the grown-ups were doing, provided we didn't do it on the same beach, and provided we didn't do it in deep water. Then somebody . . . Irene, I think . . . remembered that the grown-ups had been drinking, and if we were about to do the same thing *they* were doing, *we'd* have to drink a little before going down to the water."

"You sure knew some nice kids," Tish said.

"Well, we were all very excited," Sandy said. "It was two o'clock in the morning, and we could hear the grown-ups laughing down there on the beach, and getting drunk seemed like a very good idea to all of us."

"*Did* you get drunk?"

"We did. That's the point of the story."

"I fail to see the point," Tish said.

"She's not finished yet," Trate said impatiently.

"We took a bottle of scotch from the bar in the living room, and went down to a little beach about a hundred yards from where the grown-ups were laughing and yelling and having their race. We were all in bathing suits, and it was very cold, and I was beginning to shake all over. Irene kept poking me in the belly and saying somebody as fat as I was shouldn't be shivering, and I kept thinking I was going to get her in the water and drown her."

"Every time you *say* that . . ."

"Come on, Tish, they were just kids."

"The fifteen-year-olds got bored and went off looking for boys. The twelve-year-olds took two or three swigs from the bottle and passed out cold. Irene and I sat in the sand alone and drinking, she trying to get up the courage to go into the water, which we knew was freezing, and I getting up the courage to drown her. Around the bend in the beach, the grown-ups were having a high old time. We drank and we drank. Irene began to forget why she'd suggested the race. I began to forget I wanted to drown her. In fact, and this is what's so funny about the story, in no time at all we discovered we had a lot in common and that we'd wasted half the summer fighting with each other when all along we might have been good friends. We ended up singing 'Auld Lang Syne' and staggering up the narrow wooden steps that led from the beach to the house, and passing out on the back porch. It was a great night. We were friends for the rest of the summer."

"Sandy," David said dead-panned, "that has *got* to be the funniest story I've ever heard in my life."

"It's a nice story," Mary Margaret said quietly.

"I thought you'd appreciate it," Sandy said.

"I don't get it," Trate said. "What's so funny about it?"

"Are you still friends?" Tish asked.

"Who?"

"You and Irene."

"No," Sandy said quickly. "She drowned last year at Coney Island."

Mary Margaret burst out laughing, slapping the tabletop with one of her delicate hands and almost knocking over the pitcher of beer.

"I don't think *that's* funny, either," Tish said.

"Mary Margaret?" Sandy said, leaning forward.

"Yes, Sandy?"

"Want to ski with us tomorrow?"

"How do I know you won't try to drown me?" Mary Margaret said, and smiled.

"No water up there," Sandy said, and returned the smile.

"Then, I guess I'm safe," Mary Margaret said.

ME: She was safe. I thought she was safe.

KR: What made you think so?

ME: We had moved inland. Away from the water.

KR: I don't understand.

ME: There was no water in the forest, don't you see? Rhoda was afraid of water. Her mother had drowned. We even had to teach her to swim.

KR: Were you afraid she might drown?

ME: No. Yes. I don't know. But the sea was very rough that day, and I guess I was glad when she refused to come in the water with us. I didn't expect anything to happen in the forest. I thought she'd be safe in the forest.

KR: But something did happen.

ME: Yes.

KR: Are you sorry about what happened?

ME: It wasn't our fault.

Christmas Eve dawned grayly and chillingly.

I had rested badly, tossing and turning with my satchel-full-of-hair dream, and felt fatigued upon awakening. I might have slept better had I accepted Alice's invitation of the night before, but by the time the three of us left the lounge at a quarter to twelve, I had no desire to talk to her (no less cater to her bizarre needs) and went directly to bed. A broken promise, as a sage once remarked, is like a broken leg.

Following Sandy's lead, we were courteous and charming to Mary Margaret during breakfast. Sandy's efforts to be friendly were all the more surprising since she normally was about as animated and talkative as a tortoise during the morning meal. This morning, however, she rattled on about the Trates and Max, and about how penetrating and directly honest Mary

Margaret's observations had been, even if she hadn't much cared for the implication that David and I were queer . . .

"I was just trying to get a rise out of you," Mary Margaret said.

Yes, but even allowing such childish motivation, Sandy felt that equating us with faggot preppies was going a bit far, although the parallel was probably lost on Trate . . .

"No, I think he got it," Mary Margaret said.

The point being that if we'd been mistaken about Foderman's accident, the sensible thing was to discuss it openly and correct any misapprehensions, rather than slinging mud at each other in the presence of outsiders, especially outsiders of *their* caliber.

"I hope you guys realize," Mary Margaret said, "that it *was* an accident. I really did panic when I saw him spread across the trail that way."

Since I was the one who'd most closely witnessed the collision, I felt compelled to point out to Mary Margaret that she had gone into a racing position, head down, knees bent, poles back . . .

"I was getting ready to jump over him," Mary Margaret said.

"Then why didn't you?" I asked.

"I told you. I panicked. I didn't think I could clear his leg."

"In any case," Sandy said, "I think we *all* reacted too strongly. *We* shouldn't have accused you, and *you* shouldn't have retaliated the way you did."

"I don't really think you guys are fags," Mary Margaret said, and smiled.

"I can offer empirical evidence to the contrary," Sandy said, and smiled back at her.

"Is it settled, then?"

"It's settled."

"I mean, I hope it's clear that . . ."

"Perfectly clear," Sandy said.

"I want to make this perfectly clear," David said.

Grinning, Mary Margaret said, "You know, I think we really *can* be friends."

"Why not?" Sandy said.

"I'm so touched I could weep," David said.

"You sure you two don't want to be alone?" I said.

"Let's go find some real live wires, Peter."

"Let's go find some real hot numbers."

"They are so clever, ho-ho," Sandy said.

In just such a cheerful mood, we left for the north face.

KR: Have you changed your mind about going west?

ME: No. What do you mean? Why should I have changed my mind?

KR: Then the trip is still on. As planned.

ME: Of course it is.

KR: I'll be frank with you, Peter . . .

ME: Have you ever been anything less?

KR: I was hoping you wouldn't go.

The top of the mountain was covered with low-hanging clouds that shrouded the unloading platform, obfuscating trees and terrain, touching our faces with cold, wet tendrils. The four of us stood in the shifting gray fog and debated taking the chair back to the bottom, rather than risking the downhill trails when visibility was so poor. Mary Margaret argued that she knew the mountain well enough to ski it blindfolded, and besides (as revealed on the chair ride up) the visibility was better just a little bit further down. She would take the lead, she said, and we could all follow in a line immediately behind her, tips to tails, until we got below the cloud cover. Please understand that none of us was in the slightest concerned about what Mary Margaret would think of our courage or skill; I mean, the hell with her, we weren't up there to impress her.

But a skier who rides to the top of a mountain is reluctant to admit he's afraid to ski down; the embarrassment of choosing descent by chair instead is equivalent to what one might feel if he walked to the end of a diving board and then refused to jump into the pool. Mary Margaret had proved to us yesterday that she knew the mountain well. We had no reason to believe that, skiing in single file behind her, we would not be led safely to the bottom today. Besides, as she had pointed out, only the very uppermost portion of the mountain was in clouds; the terrain below was free of fog and could be skied with ease. We decided to trust her. As promised, she took the lead. Sandy was directly behind her, the tips of her skis almost touching Mary Margaret's tails ahead. David was next. I was last in line.

ME: If this is going to be another lecture . . .

KR: I wasn't aware that I'd been lecturing you.

ME: You just did a twenty-minute number on narcissism and self-approval and nonrelating and entirely impersonal personal relationships. Wasn't that a lecture? Gee, *I* thought it was a lecture.

KR: What I'm about to say is not a lecture. You probably won't enjoy hearing it, but it must be said anyway. I'd feel derelict, if I didn't express my . . .

ME: How'd this get so serious all of a sudden?

KR: It's been serious all along.

ME: You're going to tell me I'm a schizophrenic, right? You're going to suggest I be committed at once before . . .

KR: No.

ME: Then, what?

KR: I'm going to ask you to stay home. Let David and Sandy go alone. Let them go, Peter.

ME: I already told you I'm going with them.

KR: I think the trip could be dangerous for you.

ME: Dangerous? Don't make me laugh.

I could barely see the tails of David's skis. I could not see David himself, I could not see Sandy ahead of him, and I certainly could not see Mary Margaret in the lead. I had the feeling I was moving through one of those movie sequences (yes, Dr. Crackers, I know, I know) where phony clouds produced by dry ice float up from below, shifting and swirling where angels fearlessly tread in the company of recently deceased heavenly candidates who can't believe they're really dead. The long black length of my skis appeared only occasionally through patches in the mist, my boots sometimes visible but most often not, the terrain itself effectively camouflaged in the roiling white and gray fog. Each shadowless, shrouded, separate bump in the trail registered as a total surprise, the shock rumbling up into my knees, my balance constantly threatened. From below, Mary Margaret called encouragement and warning, "Easy, guys, we're getting there," or "Watch it, bad bump!" or "Keep loose, feel the terrain," or "Trees ahead, stay close!" I had once read a newspaper article about a blind skier (yes, *blind!*) who used a seeing-eye dog to lead him down the mountain, the dog having a small bell attached to a collar around his neck. At the time, I made some wise-ass remark about the blind man being just your regular garden variety skier, but the dog being an absolute whiz. The story did not seem so funny to me now. Mary Margaret was our radar and our sonar, guiding us down and through the suffocating cloud, "Sharp left," her voice reassuring, "We're coming to some moguls," her skill unquestioned, "We'll traverse this, stick together," her knowledge of the mountain totally reliable.

We stopped to rest by the side of the trail after we had crossed the field of moguls, huddling close as the fog swirled around us, an enveloping specter that seemed to have been summoned from some cold, dank crypt to which it was eager now to drag us.

"Everybody okay?" Mary Margaret asked.

"Yeah," Sandy said briefly.

"We'll be out of this soon," Mary Margaret said. "The worst part is just ahead. Let's stick very close together. Okay?"

KR: We're making progress here, Peter, you're coming to a better understanding of yourself. But I don't think you yet realize how threatening the relationship between you, Sandy, and . . .

ME: I don't find it threatening.

KR: It's threatening because it keeps alive this concept of infantile omnipotence.

ME: I don't know what that means.

KR: It means that *together* you feel you can do whatever you want to do and get away with it.

ME: That's ridiculous.

KR: Isn't that what happened with Rhoda? You destroyed her and then . . .

ME: *Destroyed* her! Jesus!

KR: Yes. You destroyed her, and you got away with it. There was no punishment, there was only reward— a tightening of the bond between the three of you, a confirmation of your omnipotence. Well, you're *not* all-powerful, Peter. You're three very troubled youngsters who . . .

ME: I don't want to hear this.

KR: I know you don't. I'd like you to listen anyway. Your occasional contact with the other two . . .

ME: Don't call them "the other two"! We're not accomplices! We have names!

KR: Have you?

ME: Yes. Sandy, David, and me.

KR: I didn't hear *your* name.

ME: Don't make it sound as if I don't exist without them!

KR: I would *like* you to exist without them. Don't go on this trip. The three of you together again for an extended period of . . .

ME: We're *always* together.

KR: No. You see each other only occasionally, you nourish your conglomerate ego only enough to sustain it. It has, in a sense, been latent since that summer five years ago. I wouldn't like to see it emerge again full-blown. Peter?

ME: I'm listening.

KR: Please don't go on this trip.

ME: I'm going.

KR: Must we risk everything we've accomplished so far?

ME: Jesus Christ, what the hell do you think can possibly *happen?*

KR: The same thing that happened five years ago.

ME: Rhoda won't be with us, Doctor. Remember?

KR: You'll find another Rhoda.

ME: One Rhoda was enough, thanks.

KR: I would hope so. That's why I'm begging you to stay home. I don't think you can survive another victim.

ME: Well, this has all been very illuminating, Doctor. I'm certainly glad you decided to speed me on my way by suggesting that my friends and I are hatchet murderers.

KR: I suggested nothing of the sort. Nor am I concerned with your friends, who might do well to seek psychiatric help of their own. I'm concerned only with *you.* *You're* my patient. If you act-out another of your . . .

ME: Here we go with the acting-out again.

KR: I hope not. Because this time you might destroy someone other than your intended victim.

ME: Who?

KR: Yourself.

We were on one of those treacherous trails that clung to the edge of the mountain, four feet wide, a sheer drop on our left. We inched down it slowly, checking constantly to regulate our speed. We could not see the chasm below; I didn't know whether or not I was grateful for that. Mary Margaret, in the lead, kept shouting directions back to us. I was convinced (or at least I was praying) that once we got through this winding passage, we would be in the clear.

"Hold it," Mary Margaret said.

Ahead of me, David checked sharply, eased up, and then slid to a gentle stop where Sandy and Mary Margaret were standing against the mountain wall. I followed his maneuver and joined them. Mary Margaret was taking off her gloves.

"My hands are freezing up," she said. "Just a second, okay?" Tucking both gloves under her arm, she brought her hands to her mouth and began blowing on them. "I think this is the end of it," she said. "There's a glade just beyond the next turn, and then we'll be out of the clouds. Everybody okay?"

"Why'd you break Foderman's leg?" Sandy asked suddenly.

"What?" Mary Margaret said, startled. One of her gloves slipped from under her arm. She stooped to retrieve it, bending at the knees, looking up at Sandy in surprise.

"You heard me, honey," Sandy said.

"I thought we . . ."

"Yeah, *what'd* you think?" David said.

Mary Margaret stood up immediately. The fog swirled around us, hiding the cliff edge not three feet from where we were pressed against the wall of snow. "You're kidding me," she said, and grinned.

"Uh-uh," Sandy said.

"You can tell us, honey," David said. "You really *did* do it on purpose, didn't you?"

"I already told you . . ."

"Yeah, but that was bullshit, wasn't it?"

"I tried to jump over him . . ."

"No, no, no, honey, you're a good jumper, don't give us that."

"I panicked."

"Sure, you did," Sandy said.

"That's the truth," Mary Margaret said. "Peter," she said, "you know that's the truth, don't you? You saw what happened."

"Yes," I said. "I saw what happened. You skied right through him. You *wanted* to break his leg."

"So what?" Mary Margaret said in sudden defiance. "Who cares about that silly Jew bastard?"

"We care about him," Sandy said.

"We care a lot," David said.

"We care enormously," I said.

She was hurrying to put on her gloves now. I think she was afraid of us. I think she was afraid we might throw her over the edge or something. I think she figured this was some kind of kangaroo Nuremberg court that had found her guilty and was now about to punish her. Her green eyes were wide with fright. The whole thing was kind of amusing. I mean, what the hell, we weren't going to shove her off the goddamn mountain! But her fear was exciting. I watched it flashing in her eyes, and I could hardly keep a smile off my face. She had the right glove on now, and was fumbling with the left, right hand clutching the woolen cuff of the other glove, gorgeous naked left hand thrusting into the fur-lined mouth, when suddenly the glove slipped from her grasp and fell to the snow an inch from the edge of the precipice. She hesitated before stooping for it, convinced that we would push her over the edge if she placed herself in such a vulnerable position. It was really funny. Her fear of us was really funny.

"Go ahead," Sandy said, "pick it up."

"You'll freeze your sweet little hand," David said.

"Listen, you guys," Mary Margaret said. "Cut it out, will you?"

"Cut what out?" I said.

"Pick up your fucking glove!" Sandy said.

Slowly, cautiously, Mary Margaret bent at the knees and reached for the glove. It was difficult to see exactly what happened next because of the fog swirling around us. The whole thing happened very quickly, and it might not have happened if Mary Margaret had been standing erect. In fact, when you consider what an experienced skier she was, the risk she took was stupid, reckless, and dangerous. We were, after all, clinging to a narrow trail on the very edge of the mountain. She should not have crouched over her skis that way, clutching one pole stuck in the snow, and leaning out precariously with her free hand in an effort to reach that glove so close to the edge.

Sandy merely lost her balance. People often lose their balance, you know, and bump into another person, or lean against him, or fall against him, or get their skis tangled, or whatever. It happens all the time, and there are never very serious consequences. But Mary Margaret was all bent over, and leaning out besides—she simply shouldn't have been trying to get that idiotic glove! And when Sandy lost her balance, her outside ski slipped from under her, and it hit Mary Margaret's inside ski, and this slight contact, because of Mary Margaret's position, was enough to set her in motion.

David grabbed Sandy's parka just in time, pulling her back as she slid toward the edge, slamming her hard against the wall. But Mary Margaret was too close to the edge for us to reach and, hunched back in a sitting position over her skis, could perform no maneuver to stop her sudden forward lurch. "Jesus," she said, and tried to stop herself by sitting completely, but by that time her behind was halfway over, her naked left hand still extended and clutching to the ski pole sunk into the snow, the strap looped around her wrist. "Jesus," she said again, softly, and went over, pulling the ski pole with her. She made no sound as she fell. She did not scream, she did not call for help. She simply disappeared into the fog. The mountain was still. We stood pressed against the wall behind us, breathing harshly. David moved cautiously toward the edge, and Sandy whispered, "Careful."

"Can you see her?" I asked.

"No," he said.

"Mary Margaret!" I shouted to the mist below. "Mary Margaret! Mary Margaret!" and my voice echoed from the shrouded rocks, bounced from boulder to boulder as Mary Margaret herself must have done on her downward plunge, the name reverberating in the abyss, "Mary Margaret, Mary Margaret," overlapping and dissipating, "Mary Margaret," and then becoming lost completely in the fog.

"We'd better get the Ski Patrol," David said.

"I'll take the lead," Sandy said, and we started down.

We went to see Foderman after dinner that night. He was lying in bed with his right leg in traction, a drug-glazed look on his face. I'm not at all sure he understood everything we told him about the accident. We explained exactly how it had happened. We explained the way Mary Margaret had leaned out dangerously close to the edge, and how Sandy had lost her balance and had almost gone over herself. We explained all of it. We told him, too, that the Ski Patrol had found her crushed and lifeless body sixty feet below the trail on a pile of jagged rock. She had broken her legs, her back, her neck, and the wrists of both beautiful hands.

When Foderman heard this, he nodded and whispered, "Good."

The ski instructors came down the slope closest to the Lodge at ten minutes to midnight. It had begun snowing again, and we stood huddled together, our arms around each other, watching them as they started down from the top. They were all carrying flares held high over their heads. From where we stood, the skiers were invisible. We saw only the red flares glowing against the blackness, like lights on a Christmas tree, strung across the mountain in a curving line.

"Look at them," David said.

"Hug me," Sandy said, "I'm freezing."

On the mountain, the instructors carved linked turns, the flares blazing in the wind. Snowflakes lazily sifted down from the sky. All was hushed.

"You'd never catch me skiing at night," I said.

"Why not?"

"Scare me to death."

"That's what you've got a shrink for, man," David said. "Get rid of all your fears."

"I'm not sure I'll be going back to him," I said.

"First sensible idea I've heard all week," David said.

"Shrinks are for crazy people," Sandy said.

"You crazy, dolling?" David asked.

"Who, me?" I said. "It's Crackers who's nuts."

"Then let *him* go find a shrink," David said.

"Hug me, hug me," Sandy said.

The instructors were almost to the bottom now. The bells in the church steeple began tolling the midnight hour, the red flares spurted luminescent blood on the hillside. Our arms around each other, the snow gently falling, we watched the skiers gliding closer and closer, and listened to the bonging bells, and suddenly grinned and hugged each other tightly.

It was Christmas morning, and all was right with the world.